"My child!" Caird exploded. "When I think what I've missed!"

He went on to add painfully, "You realize what you've done me out of, woman? Half her childhood...."

"She was never yours!" Annabel argued wildly, the years of loneliness sweeping her away. "All you did was enjoy yourself for a few weeks, ten years ago."

"So, I lose a daughter and my daughter loses a father," Caird snapped back. "And that's all right? You didn't need to find out the truth?"

"What was I supposed to do, hang around until you'd got rid of your wife again?" Annabel glared up at him.

"I spent over a year looking for you," Caird responded in tones measurably subdued. "Do you know that, Bel?" he almost whispered. "I won't lose you again, not now."

JESSICA MARCHANT, a retired English teacher, and her ex-diplomat husband, Peter, have no children but enjoy a wonderful life, traveling extensively. Her first book was drawn from one such journey across Europe. They have lived all over the world, but at present reside in Exeter in Devon.

JESSICA MARCHANT

journey of discovery

Harlequin Books

TORONTO • NEW YORK • LONDON
AMSTERDAM • PARIS • SYDNEY • HAMBURG
STOCKHOLM • ATHENS • TOKYO • MILAN

Harlequin Presents first edition February 1989
ISBN 0-373-11145-2

Original hardcover edition published in 1988
by Mills & Boon Limited

CHAPTER ONE

TRUST Caird Gloster to be up here in the teeth of the wind!

Annabel clung to the bulkhead, weaker at the knees than ever, wishing she were anywhere but on this cross-Channel ferry, wishing the solitary figure at the rail were anybody else. He had his back to her, but she couldn't mistake him, not Caird. In ten years he had lost none of the tough, athletic watchfulness that showed now in the way he stood, weight well forward, long legs tense in spite of the easy lines of his wide shoulders. Wherever he was, Caird Gloster was always ready for action.

She thought of turning back before he could see her, but the seasickness which had brought her out here was worse now. So she struggled to the other rail, cotton jacket flattened to the slender lines of her body, fair hair tugging away from her face. She had nearly made it when a grip on both her arms caught her back. Feebly resisting, she felt herself pulled round to face him.

'Annabel Blythe, by all that's wonderful!' the remembered voice vibrated in her ear. 'What are you . . .' He broke off, scanning her face, summing her up as he always had and knowing at once what was wrong. 'Not into the wind, silly. Do you want it back all over yourself?'

Unable to reply, unable to speak at all, she let herself be hustled to the leeward rail. Then her digestive system took over, and she knew nothing at all except a huge relief as the horrible, everything-going-the-wrong-way feeling died away. It left her weak and queasy still, but she could cope with that. What she couldn't cope with was Caird, holding her so tenderly that she wanted nothing but to collapse against him. His great bulk was protecting her from the worst of the wind, his muscular arms steadied her against the rail with a comforting pressure that was already helping her stomach to right itself.

'Is that it, then?'

The deep voice was in her ear again, so close she could feel the warmth of his breath. She gazed ahead at the grey, shifting horizon, closed her eyes and, with enormous effort, nodded. None of this seemed to be happening to her any more. Somewhere, a long way off, her body was being half-walked, half-carried to a bench by the bulkhead, made to sit down, pulled against a solid shoulder. It was so strong, that shoulder, such a good place for her to rest her head and forget what its owner had done to her.

She had imagined this meeting so often. She would be at a party, her short hair grown long and dazzlingly blonde, her blue eyes suddenly wide enough and deep enough to drown all the men who were competing for a glance from them. Or—another favourite—she would be dining in a sophisticated restaurant with just one distinguished, enraptured admirer. She knew it was silly, but that was how it had taken her at the time. What she'd longed for most in those early miserable months had been the chance to get back at him, to treat him as he'd treated her, to show him that she, too, could have somebody else.

The trouble was, the somebody elses had been such shadowy figures. After Caird, most men had seemed shadowy to her. She had thrown herself into her work instead, and in the steadily growing demand for her catering, new problems and new achievements and new prosperity, those childish revenge fantasies had troubled her less and less. She could hardly say she'd forgotten Caird, no chance of that, but she'd adjusted. In the humdrum routine of building up a small business in a small town, she'd had little time to watch or listen to his programme, and had seen no reason why their paths should ever cross again.

Only now they had, and the feeling that she ought to be grateful for his practical help made it all the worse. Grateful, indeed! She straightened up, glad her anti-seasickness pill had started working at last, and called on the discipline which had seen her through those early terrible years. All right, just now he'd been useful—but what was that, compared to the misery he'd caused her, all she had to endure alone because of him? She rose and found she could stay on her feet—indeed, was stronger than she'd hoped.

'Thanks——' she began, but the wind howled her down and she had to continue at a shout. 'See you . . .' She turned away.

'Oh, no, you don't!' He grabbed her arms again.

She must be feeling better. She could set her teeth now and stiffen away from him, concentrating on how much she hated him and ignoring the other emotions the contact was rousing in her.

'Let me go, please.'

'Just like that?' the deep voice cut through the wind so that she could hear the incredulity in it. 'Let you disappear for another ten years?'

'As if that ever bothered you . . . '

'How do you know what bothers me and what doesn't? You ran out on me, remember?'

'I ran out on . . . '

Annabel stopped, helpless against the cool arrogance of the man. After what he'd done! She wrenched her arms free, but he only captured her hand instead, and she knew then with something like despair that nothing had changed. Every nerve in her body leapt into action, her heart hammered louder than the engines beneath their feet, her blood surged like the lifting sea. Stiff with the fury of her inner resistance, but outwardly calm, she faced him again.

'I won't ask where you're heading,' his big voice dominated hers without effort, 'because you won't tell me. But until Calais I've got you and I'm keeping you.'

She squared her shoulders. 'And just what are you going to do with me?'

'What I'd have done ten years ago, if you'd let me. Talk.'

She tried a dry laugh, but it was lost in the wind. Really, this was hopeless! He wasn't dealing with a forlorn, affection-hungry eighteen-year-old any more, and the sooner he knew it the better, but how could she show him her hard-won poise when she was having to scream at the top of her voice? To make things worse, the next squall of rain had bustled right over them.

'Great!' she shouted. 'You talk, and we get pneumonia.'

'My Bel never used to worry about things like that . . . '

'*Your Bel*,' she fought the wind for the bitter emphasis she needed, 'doesn't exist any more. Thanks partly to you.'

'You surely don't think I wanted . . . '

'What I think's my business.' She tried to free her hand. 'Will you kindly let go of me?'

'Not a chance.'

She bit her lip. 'Then at least let's stay dry.'

'After you.' Keeping tight hold of her, Caird pushed her to the heavy bulkhead door, wrenched it open, and stepped after her over the high sill. 'This way.'

She shot a hasty glance across the rows of reclining chairs. Sian was still in her corner, calmly eating her sandwiches and reading her book—no problems of seasickness for Sian. Let her be, then—with luck, she and Caird wouldn't have to meet at all. He had found them a place by the window on the opposite side, and was now standing back to let Annabel go in first. So he was able to combine courtesy with caution, she thought ironically, and put her where she wouldn't be able to leave without climbing over him. She sat down and watched the spray dashing the other side of the salty glass, sensing with every pore of her body him settling beside her, folding his legs into the space that would have been adequate for most passengers. Suddenly, they might have been alone on the boat. The tall back-rests of the seats in front cut off their vision and muffled the everyday noises of the saloon, so that she was again conscious of the knock of the engines, the hissing, growling sea, the tumult inside her own body.

'Now, Annabel Blythe,' he began at once, 'is it any good if I apologise?'

'Whatever for?' She was glad of the sea-noise to cover the shakiness of the words she meant to be so dismissive. 'You did me a favour, letting me find out the truth about you . . . '

'Come off it!' His voice was hard. 'Don't pull that phoney patter on me, darling, I won't have it . . . '

'And don't you dare call me darling!'

'That's more like it.' Caird settled back, satisfied. 'That's my Annabel talking now.'

'No, it isn't.' She turned to glare, then looked hastily away, because he was so much more attractive than she had chosen to remember him.

She could see now that over the years she had gradually adapted her memories to suit her needs. He was a heartless, self-indulgent cheat, so she had to debase him in her mind, remember and exaggerate whatever might be wrong with his looks. So she'd been sure that, at thirty-seven, his bulk must be running to fat, his carelessness with clothes degenerating to mere slovenliness. Only they weren't. His weight was still all muscle, and he carried it as lightly as ever, with quick reflexes and springy movements. His clothes were still perfectly respectable, simply the clothes of a man who wasn't very interested in what he wore. It couldn't possibly be the same leather jacket and shapeless dark cords he'd had ten years ago, but they looked the same and were probably bought the same way—off the peg in a hurry. Even the open-necked shirt hadn't changed much, he'd favoured those comfortable cottons long before they were in fashion. And his brown hair was still too long, not stylish long but just forgetting-to-have-it-cut long, and tangled now as the wind had left it.

Worse, far worse, was being forced to notice the things she'd blotted out of her mind altogether. She glanced at him again and, yes, the hazel eyes were steady as ever. They had little lines now that rayed up from the corners, but that only made him seem kinder—more of a sham, she reminded herself mercilessly. Well, the years might have added to his authority, but they hadn't let him off scot-free—somebody had broken his nose. How infuriating that the crooked line of it only added to his attractiveness!

Caird was looking straight at her now, another of the habits she'd preferred to forget. She'd never felt able to hide anything from him; he'd always gone straight through her surface pretences to her innermost thoughts. She imagined that happening all over again, and hastily assured herself it was only fancy.

'You amaze me, Caird!' Her dry laugh worked much better this time. 'Why try and talk yourself out of trouble that went away ten years ago . . . '

'You're doing it again. Now stop!'

'Right,' she compressed her lips, 'let me past, then, please.'

For goodness' sake, Bel!' He ran a hand through his hair, another half-forgotten gesture stirring a fresh host of memories. 'How are we ever going to to put ourselves right if you pull this society-hostess act . . . '

'I'm not pulling any act,' she retorted, stung. 'And there's nothing to put right . . . '

'Oh, yes, there is! I know how badly I hurt you . . . '

'Water under the bridge,' she countered quickly —did he think she'd been sitting in a corner and pining for him ever since? 'I'm surprised you even remember.'

'Don't kid yourself. I still have nightmares about it.'

Nightmares. Yes, she had those herself, even now. That summer in Torquay. The new signature in the hotel register— M.E. Gloster. The bed she had come to think of as hers and his with a suitcase on it, with a beautiful red-haired woman unpacking the suitcase. The sudden sickening knowledge that this woman had a better right to Caird than she had.

' . . . never seen anyone look so . . . so lost . . . as you did then.' His voice brought her out of it. 'I couldn't think of anything else for weeks.'

'So you had a bad conscience.' Stirred by the

vividness of her memories, Annabel spoke with more heat than she had intended. 'Big deal.'

'Millie was always doing things on the spur of the moment like that. I'd no idea she was coming . . . '

'I'll bet you hadn't'!' She turned her head sharply. One of the many miseries of that terrible time had been her mental picture of Caird with his wife, explaining away her intrusion. In spite of herself, she had to ask, 'So that was her name?'

'That was Millie.' He gently pulled a strand of the short hair at the back of her neck.

How could she have forgotten this particular caress, so teasing, so protective, so ultimately false! She jerked her head away. 'Don't do that.'

'Sorry. She was upset, too . . . '

'Spare me the details,' she rapped, as each word stabbed a little nearer the old torment.

'In fact, that was why she . . . ' His eyes held hers, a frown drawing the shaggy brows together over the top of that fighter's nose.

'She what?'

'Nothing. It was all a long time ago.'

She wrenched her gaze away, tried to rest it instead on the leaping, splashing water, then in desperation on the grubby cover of the seat in front. She wasn't going to let him see how clearly it all came back to her, ten years or not.

She'd known, of course, that she wasn't the first. In those days, wanting so much to make him completely her own, she had probed eagerly, hungrily, anxious to absorb every detail of his experience, however much it hurt. He hadn't allowed that or anything like it, but she had been able to build up a picture of the life he led as an investigative reporter. The tenseness and the adrenalin, the strange people and places. Of course there had been women, but none who meant anything to him now. All right then, perhaps a fond memory or two.

Her heart twisted with bitterness. He'd seemed so open and straightforward telling her that, instead of what he really was— faithless, disloyal, two-faced. Why had he never told her he was married? It changed the whole picture, threw a new, ugly light on everything that had happened between them, his tenderness and his understanding . . . She swallowed hard, determined not to let herself think about that.

'Are you all right?' Caird surveyed her with a frown. 'Perhaps we should go back on deck again.'

She realised with surprise that he was talking about her seasickness. When had it stopped bothering her?' She supposed it had just gradually gone as this other, deeper sickness took over, the greater pain driving out the less.

'I'll survive.' She turned angrily away, rejecting his concern, and found she could look out to sea now without the least discomfort. 'One of the things you taught me.'

'Oh, my dear!'

She jerked round to look at him again, stung by the compassion in his tone. The hazel eyes saw deep as ever into her own; it was almost as if he knew what she'd been through.

'Save your pity!' Was that her voice, hissing like

a cat? She drew a long breath and forced some control into it. 'I read you were divorced. Your . . . Millie . . . what happened to her?'

'Skip it.' A wide, good-natured gesture, and his ex-wife was consigned to his past, where they all belonged. 'If it's any consolation to you, she wiped the floor with me.'

'Good. I only wish it had been me doing that.'

'So do I, Bel. So do I.' Could he really be as wistful, as regretful as he sounded? 'Though you did your share, disappearing like that. I had a lot of thinking to do . . . '

'Not before time.'

He winced, shrugged, went on evenly, 'Taking stock . . . '

'It must have been a nasty experience.'

He gave her a long look, then seemed to come to a decision. 'You're spoiling for a fight, then?'

'Certainly not!' But even as she made the denial she found she was catching her breath, straightening her back, raising her chin so she could fix him with a scornful sideways glance. 'I wouldn't lower myself . . . '

'Then supposing you stop making silly, smart remarks, and listen to what I'm trying to tell you?'

'No, *you* listen, Caird Gloster. So you feel bad about . . . what you did. Is that supposed to make it better for me?'

He wasn't put down as she'd hoped, not at all. Instead, he was just staring at her, and in that stare she was suddenly conscious of things about her appearance she hadn't thought of in years. The way she always cut her own hair to save time, and never bothered with make-up for the same reason. The flat-heeled shoes and sensible, boring jacket and trousers she'd chosen for travelling. She felt the heat rising in her cheeks, and told herself it was rage at this cool inspection of her, but she knew it wasn't as simple as that. Hard as it was to admit, she would have liked to have been prepared for this meeting, to have been able to shine herself up a bit, dress more expensively and show that life was treating her well. She made a move to hide her work-worn hands, but on second thoughts spread them open on her lap. She wasn't going to be ashamed of the reason for her success.

They gave her courage, those hands. They brought her back to the here and now, to efficient Annabel Stroud, employer of labour, negotiator of contracts, hard-headed businesswoman. Somewhere inside her, a lonely, bewildered girl was still crying, beating against her hard-won composure like the sea beating the glass, but the cries were fainter now, as the sea was calmer.

'You've come on, you know.'

She couldn't mistake the admiration in the words, yet she bristled. 'Don't you condescend to me!'

'You always were liable to get your rag out . . .'

'And you always tried to flatter your way out of it.'

'No flattery, Annabel Blythe. So you still don't know what a traffic-stopper you are?'

She threw up her head impatiently. Traffic-stopper, indeed! In the summer, when the sun bleached her hair and her tan made her eyes seem bluer, some men did try to chat her up, but that happened to most women, just as most women were whistled at from building sites and passing lorries. She'd never taken it seriously, and when he'd praised her looks ten years ago she hadn't taken that seriously, either.

Certainly, at the time she'd believed he meant it as far as he was concerned. In the years that followed, she'd forced herself to face her own stupidity over that, just to make sure she wasn't fooled again, and she hadn't been. But during those few weeks she'd really believed that for him she was beautiful. More fool her—surely he wasn't going to try that one again?

'Same old line,' she jeered. 'Isn't it a bit tired by now?'

'No line, Bel.'

'Whatever it is, I don't want to know.'

He sighed and slumped back, eyes staring unseeingly ahead. 'It's worse than I thought.'

'No, it isn't. She didn't know why she rushed to contradict him like that. After all, it *was* worse than he thought—much worse. But something in his tone, some implied criticism, set her teeth on edge. 'I'm doing fine . . . '

'Oh, sure! And you're also trying to be hard as nails.'

'You won't fool me twice, if that's what you think.'

'I'm not trying to fool you, only . . . ' He shrugged, as near helplessness as she'd ever seen him. 'Only put right some of the damage between us . . . but I can see it's too late for that.'

'Much too late,' agreed Annabel, and then wished she hadn't spoken so hastily. It was there again, that criticism, and somehow she seemed to have confirmed it.

'Yes,' he was nodding wearily, 'you are what you are, and if any of that's my fault, it's no good being sorry now.'

She stiffened again at his presumption. 'Do you think because you once picked me up and put me down, my life changed——'

She stopped in confusion at having so unthinkingly told the simple truth, Knowing him had done just that, changed her life for ever, only nothing on earth was going to persuade her to tell him about that. She really must watch her tongue.

She glanced at her watch. 'All right, Caird, is your conscience straight now? Because I have to . . . '

Have to what? She wasn't going to tell her real reason for wanting to get away, and her sluggish brain was refusing to invent one. She drummed her feet on the dusty brown lino, more angry with herself than with him. She was letting him throw her, playing into his hands—he'd already seen she was hiding something. All his newshound instincts were alerted now, the deep-set eyes drilling through her.

'You're in a hurry?'

She bristled at the ironic tone, but she knew what he meant. On a cross-Channel ferry, you couldn't go anywhere very much as long as you were at sea. 'I'd like to clean myself up.'

'At the wash-basins, you mean? He sounded genuinely surprised, as he added,'Haven't you done this kind of crossing before?'

She was silenced. She had no intention of going near the wash basins—in fact, meant to give them as wide a berth as possible. The number of seasick passengers in there was the reason she had gone on deck in the first place.

'You're travelling alone?' he asked as if it had just occurred to him.

She bunched her left hand against her jacket. 'You've been pretty sure of that till now.'

'You were in quite a state, love. If there had been anybody, surely he'd have been with you?'

'Will you come out of the past, for goodness' sake?' Her hackles had risen anew at the casual endearment. 'Nobody has to hold my head when I'm seasick, I'm a big girl now.'

'You didn't look it, out there,' He glanced through the window at the looming French coastline, 'We'll be docking soon, and there's so much I wanted to say . . . you meant a lot to me, Bel.'

'Me and how many others?'

'Only you.'

She watched the water grow calmer as they came within the shelter of the land. In spite of herself, the simple words had pierced all her defences. 'It's too late for that now,' she answered, much more softly than she'd intended.

'You were so young,' the square jaw tightened, 'so dependent on me . . .'

'I was not!' She flung round, and found his eyes

uncomfortably close to her own. 'I've never depended on anybody.'

'Come off it, love.'

Caird gripped her elbow and she couldn't wrench it away. The old magic had caught her, singing in her blood, numbing her to everything except the gentle strength of his fingers, the warm friction through the cotton of her sleeve as he moved his thumb against the skin of her inner arm. She knew he was just as aware of her as she was of him. His glance had dropped to her mouth, his own lips parting in the way she remembered so well. It was useless to remind herself how he had deceived her, made love to her while he was still married to another woman. She was simply his, transfixed until he relased her with a quick breath and a startled movement of his head.

'Where was I?'

'Trying . . .' she swallowed hard, but still her tongue felt dry and clumsy as it formed the words '. . . trying to tell me I was dependent on you.'

'Oh. Yes. After you left, I found that worked two ways.'

As long as she didn't look at him, she could speak with some of her old self-control. 'Are you saying you missed me?'

'More than that.'

'And you expect me to believe that? After the way I found out about your . . .' she swallowed, forcing out the words '. . . your wife?'

He paused to reflect, and the memories came rushing back. He'd always treated her questions in just this way, answered them with a well con-

sidered honesty, as if he wanted to give himself
and his past into her keeping; that was why it hurt
so much to learn of the marriage he'd never
mentioned. And here he was again, seeming to
give a straight answer to a straight question. Only
seeming, she reminded herself sharply.

'I'd like to have told you about that, Bel, if you'd
only stayed to listen . . .'

'You mean,' she flung at him, 'given you the
chance to lie your way out of it?'

'You know damn well I never lied to you.'

She stared ahead, wanting against all common
sense to believe him. She always had believed
him . . .

She was eighteen, and starved. Not physically
hungry—working with food saw to that, she never
wanted much to eat even at mealtimes. No, it was
humanity she longed for, somebody to care about
her, somebody who might give her the love she'd
missed from her unknown father or her wild,
long-dead mother. Young and foolish as she was
then, she believed this big man with his quiet
strength could meet her need, fill the emptiness
left by her neglected childhood.

They met one afternoon during her day off. She
arrived bikini-clad in what she thought of as her
own secret corner of the hotel garden, and found
him already there, sunbathing. She saw at once
that he liked her, and because he was Caird, his
liking pleased and soothed her battered spirit. She
didn't feel threatened as she so often did when
men approached her. Instead, she warmed to the
admiration in his eyes, answered his teasing chat

as any girl might, felt more human because he was taking an interest in her.

She knew his glance was lingering on her bronzed legs, her supple hips, the soft curves of her young breasts, and she was glad. When he kissed her, there in the corner of the old kitchen garden with sun-warmed brick sheltering them in two directions, she didn't respond, but nor did she stiffen and retreat as she always had with other men. Drawn by his gentleness and his patient understanding, she happily accepted his invitation to supper that evening.

He'd taken her to the Italian restaurant by the harbour, but she hadn't wanted to eat. Only to be with him. Only to savour his quiet interest, his careful questions, the solid strength of his footsteps by her side in the darkness as they walked home.

Home! The very word reminded her of the dreary institutions she'd had to live in after her mother died. Her attic bedroom in the hotel was as good a home as any she'd had, better than most. Until then she'd been pleased with it, proud of the little touches she'd added to make it more welcoming. Only in the corridor outside Caird's room, when he'd kissed her softly on the cheek and then gathered her into his arms, only then had that attic of hers sudddenly seemed cold, desolate, empty. How could she return there, how could she leave this warmth which held and encompassed her so steadily?

Often, in the angry years that followed, she had raged at herself for letting it happen, that slow, easy progress to his room and his bed. But at the time it had seemed so natural, so right. At the time she'd wanted nothing but to stay with him, rejoice in his closeness, exchange the gift of his tenderness for the gift of her love, which she knew she had always saved for this.

When that first time was over, she'd learnt that some of it had been a new experience for him, too. He had been a little rueful, a little solemn over her lost virginity. She'd had to convince him she regretted nothing except the temporary setback to their lovemaking. The pain had been nothing, quickly forgotten in the leaping exultation of all the nights from then on, when she'd come to him and found a delight she'd never known since except in dreams.

Oh, yes, in dreams. But in those empty days and nights after she'd run away from him, it wasn't only or even chiefly the pleasure she'd missed most. Much more bitterly, she had longed for the closeness, the lazy warmth of after-love when she had lain with her head on his shoulder and rubbed her palm over the rough hair on his chest. When he had cupped her breast with the sleepy protectiveness of passion spent, and murmured those serious answers to her endless questions.

He'd wanted to know about her too, but that hadn't taken long. She wouldn't talk about the string of foster homes, but had told him something of the Grants, who had shown her true kindness while she struggled to complete her catering course, and who had helped her find the job in the hotel kitchen. She'd never visited the Grants again, after she left Torquay.

He could listen so carefully, probe so gently, understand so quickly when he strayed into one of the many painful areas of her life. She was furious with herself after for not seeing his sympathy for what it was, a part of his professional stock-in-trade. She should have recognised it, she'd met the same sympathy often enough from social workers and all the others who filled the gap where her parents should have been. But her need of him was so urgent, she had to believe he was personally interested, loved and needed her, too.

She'd been stupid, and had suffered for it. He was famous now for his probings into fraud and injustice. Time and again she'd been drawn to the radio or television set and heard, hand on the off-switch, that same professional sympathy helping bewildered victims tell their stories. And now he was trying it on her again. She closed her eyes, shook her head to clear it, and realised the boat's engines had stilled. Faint noises filtered in from the quayside.

'I'd better go.' She sprang up in a panic.

He didn't stir. 'What's your hurry? They'll call us when it's time to rejoin the cars . . . Tell me where you're heading, Bel.'

She looked wildly through the crowd, conscious of being mere seconds now from the event that would make all her problems worse. 'You said you weren't going to ask me that.'

'I've said a lot of stupid things in my time, and here's another. Travel with me, instead.'

'Please, Caird, I must go . . . ' she began, and then it was too late. She saw with sinking heart that Sian was coming to join them.

CHAPTER TWO

'YOUR bag, Mummy.' Sian handed over the shoulder-bag. 'I've put my book back in it, and the apple for later.'

The loudspeakers began their four-language instructions for passengers to rejoin their vehicles. Annabel gathered her jacket tight and made a determined movement to push by Caird, but it was useless. Knees jammed against the back of the row in front, he blocked her escape without even being aware of it. Unless she wanted to stand on her seat and jump over him, she would have to wait till he moved—and he clearly wasn't going to do that until he'd looked his fill at Sian.

The worst had happened—he'd recognised her at once. And really, how could he not? She was him in delicate miniature: stubborn little jaw, square wide-set cheekbones, bright hazel eyes full of exactly his own watchful understanding. That inherited understanding was one of the reasons why it had been impossible ever to forget Caird. In the nine years of Sian's life, she had shown herself extraordinarily like him in the way she could sum things up and reach decisions. She asked awkward questions, too; at times like this, you could almost see them coming.

'He's got a gap between his teeth, Mummy,' she observed. 'Just like mine.'

'Don't be rude,' Annabel said sharply, distracted by the stony face Caird was turning on her.

'Why didn't you tell me?' he demanded.

She shot a helpless glance round. The seats were empty, the other passengers already making their way down to the car-decks. Of all times for this to happen! She'd had so many dreams about it, night-dreams when everything went crazy, daydreams when she made any number of dry, cutting answers to the question he'd just asked. She couldn't think of any of those now.

'Please, Caird,' she urged desperately, 'we've got to go.'

But he stayed where he was, hands on the arms of the seat. They were white-knuckled, she noted, and his face showed the same tension. He had gone very pale, the easy lines of his mouth compressed, his eyes . . . she had never known his eyes like this, not in all their brief time together. Never had she seen them other than kind and teasingly good-humoured. Now a cold rage had changed their summer hazel to a concentrated wintry green. They had become hunter's eyes.

'Do you still think you can walk away from me? he demanded, fury in every sawn-off syllable. 'Just as if you hadn't my . . . ' He closed his mouth tight, and looked again to where Sian stood with her head on one side, taking it all in. Abruptly, his manner changed as he smiled and stuck out a hand. 'Hello, half-pint. Mummy didn't tell me your name.'

The child responded as any child would, and Annabel was left to marvel at Caird's self-control.

He hadn't stopped being furious, she could tell that from the hand still clenched round the arm of his seat. But he wasn't going to show it and frighten Sian. On the contrary, he was determined to make friends with her. No wonder he dealt so firmly with all those crooks he exposed in his programmes. No wonder he was so well able to calm their victims, and thus get a coherent story into his tape-recorder.

'Sian,' he was repeating now, enjoying the sturdy confidence of her answers, 'do you like being called that?'

''s all right,' Sian said indifferently. 'I'd sooner be Hayley, though. My best friend's called Hayley.'

'Is she? And where do you live, Sian?'

'Number-seven-North-Street-Rybridge-Suffolk,' Sian chanted promptly, running it off as she had been taught, in case she ever got lost.

Annabel listened in dismay and growing anger. He was taking it all in, she could tell that from his sudden stillness, and it was an easy enough address to learn by heart. *I'll move*, she fumed to herself, and had a painful picture of her beloved Victorian house, emptied of all her carefully chosen furniture and passed on to strangers. And it wouldn't work anyway. She had a business to run; she couldn't afford to hide or to change her name again. He would track her down as soon as he knew the name she had assumed after they had parted.

'Caird,' she snapped, 'we ought to be with our cars . . .'

'So you're travelling by car?'

'By Neddy.' Sian's eyes sparkled as she brought out the nickname she had coined. 'We've never had aVolkswagen before. He's just like a sweet little donkey . . . '

'And where are you going with Neddy?'

'Don't know yet. Mummy says Salzburg.'

'Caird,' Annabel glanced at the steward who had appeared in the doorway with a vacuum cleaner, 'if you don't move, I'll have to climb over you.'

'Plenty of time.' He stood up and turned his back on her, throwing over his shoulder, 'If you go too soon, you only shuffle down with the crowd.'

'And that would never do, would it?' She pushed out after him, settling her bag on her shoulder.

Sian was already on her way with Caird. 'They've got Whale Deck, and Swan Deck, and Elephant Deck,' she was telling him, and in response to his question, 'We're on Whale. By door number one, I noticed it as we came up.'

'That'll be this way, then.'

Still absorbed in Sian's chatter, he guided them to the port side of the boat. Trailing after them, fumbling in her shoulder-bag for her keys, Annabel raged anew at the way he was taking over, behaving exactly as if he were Sian's acknowledged father. Look at him, she thought, head bent as he attended so seriously to all her excited comments, big hand on her shoulder to steer her in the direction he intended them all to go. What was more, now they were both on their feet and moving, the resemblance was more conspicuous than ever. They even had the same long-legged walk, a saunter at the moment as they were slowed down by the shuffling crowd. She caught up with them in time to hear Sian's admiring comment.

'You know a lot about this boat, don't you? You said there was no hurry.'

'Here we are.' He paused at the entrance to Whale Deck, and looked across the packed ranks of cars with passengers squeezing their way between. 'Can you pick out Neddy?'

'Easy,' she pointed to the dark red Volkwagen next to the door, 'that's him. Would you like to see my keys for him?' She fished her favourite riding-crop key-ring out of her pocket, and showed it off on her small capable palm. 'That's the cap of the petrol tank, this is the door and ignition . . .'

'Off you go,' Annabel cut in. She waited till Sian had reached the car, then turned again to Caird. 'I hope you're proud of yourself. Asking the child . . .'

'My child!'

It came out so explosively that Sian looked up from unlocking the car, and stared at them, wide-eyed. Had she heard?

In spite of her worry about that, Annabel flinched at the bitterness of the words. They seemed torn from the roots of his consciousness, from some part of him which perhaps he kept hidden even from himself. She caught a brief glimpse of a pain and longing equal to any she herself had ever suffered, a depth of feeling that called to the depth of her own, and raised questions she would rather not answer.

Had she been wrong, then, not to tell him? She'd been so set on her own independence, so determined never to let him know what she was going through, that maybe it had blinded her to the possibility that he, too, could be hurt. But even as the unwanted idea formed it vanished in the need to defend herself against his hard, controlled fury;

'Sian, do as you're told,' she called, and watched with relief as the child climbed into their car.

That left Caird to deal with. Eyes opaque and unyielding, jaw set, mouth a grim line, he might have been carved in granite. 'When I think what I've missed,' his voice came out a restrained growl, 'I could strangle you.'

'How right I was not to tell you, then!' She squared up to him on the exhilarating wave of ten years' anger, ten years' worry and sleepless misery and loneliness, all sweeping her at last in the right direction, against the cause of it.

'You realise what you've done me out of, woman? Half her childhood . . .'

'And all the worry!'

'Worry?' Abruptly checked for a moment, he frowned down at her. 'She's all right, is she?'

'Of course she is!' Her reply was impatient, not so much with him as with herself for being distracted by his genuine concern. 'She never even has colds. I just meant the ordinary day-to-day worries . . .'

'D'you think I'm pleased not to have those?

D'you think it suits me to be robbed of the chance to take care of my own . . . '

'She was never yours!' Annabel's denial was all the wilder for having argued this one out so often with herself. 'All you did was enjoy yourself for a few weeks, ten years ago . . . '

'So I lose a daughter, and my daughter loses a father,' he snapped. 'And that's all right, your mind's made up, you don't need to find out the facts . . .'

'You've forgotten—I *did* find out the facts!'

'And never stopped to ask a single question. You always were a little know-all . . .'

'I was not!' She glared up at him, outraged at this new picture of herself. 'What was I supposed to do, hang round until you'd got rid of your wife again?'

'You know damn well what you should have done. Got in touch with me the minute you found you were pregnant.' The deep voice ground down her attempted answer. 'I spent a year looking for you, d'you know that?'

'You didn't have the right . . .'

'And all the time you were . . . it doesn't bear thinking about.'

'I managed.'

'Yes, and you'd have managed a hell of a lot better if I'd been able to help.'

Annabel had a sudden tremor of apprehension, of having taken on more than she bargained for. Ahead of them, something rattled, a draught of fresh air blew in among the petrol fumes, and daylight reflected from the shiny paintwork of the cars. She turned away from him with a sense of relief.

'They've lowered the ramp. We'd better go.'

'Come back here!' Caird grabbed her arms and pulled her round towards him. 'I wouldn't let you try that one an hour ago—how d'you think I feel about it now?'

'We don't want to miss our turn . . . '

'My turn or my daughter, which d'you think matters most?'

She arched away from him and looked down first at his right hand, then at his left. They were crushing her sleeves, digging into her flesh, warming it to a tingling languor that spread up her shoulders and raised the hair on the back of her neck. She made a desperate effort to distract herself.

'You certainly pick your time and place!'

He ignored the comment, pushing his own line of enquiry with all the bulldog tenacity which had made him famous. 'I want to know where you're heading. Which route?'

'You got enough out of Sian . . .'

'Where?'

It was no use struggling, she wouldn't get away until he let her. And meanwhile she had to go on inhaling this disturbing smell of wet leather and warm masculinity, fighting the weakness and longing that possessed her, pushing down her memories of that golden time when she'd loved him and had believed he loved her.

'Lille,' she said, desperately conjuring the road-map in her mind. 'We've booked a hotel in Lille.'

He seemed to relax, almost as if this were the

answer he was expecting. Yet how could it be, when she'd just made it up?

'Which one?' he asked in a tired voice.

She decided it would be all right to give him the correct name, seeing she'd given him the wrong town. 'The Voltaire.'

'See you there, then.'

His expression was hard to read as he released her, but she couldn't think about that now. She covered the short distance to her own car in dread, aware of how inquisitively Sian had been watching them through the car window. Now for another bout of shrewd, inexorable questions—if only the child wasn't so very much her father's daughter!

But she had reckoned without the excitement of a nine-year-old abroad for the first time. Sian was jumping up and down, eyes on the open ramp ahead.

'The people behind us are cross, they think we're going to stop them getting off . . .'

'Here.' Glad of the chance to distract her further, Annabel slung her bag across to the back seat. 'Find the passport, and less of your chatter.'

She started the engine just in time for the green-overalled deck hand to signal her forward. Bump up, bump down, and they were over the ramp and rolling towards the distant Customs shed. Sian put on her safety-belt and wriggled to her window to savour the rainy expanse of Calais docks.

'We're Abroad, Mummy! This is Abroad, and this is us and Neddy driving in it . . .'

'Stop fizzing and give me the passport,' Annabel commanded, and leant across to hold it out to Passport Control.

That done, she settled down to her driving. Remembering to keep to the right, looking for road signs and street names, she wondered which of these British cars fanning out of the docks was Caird's. He knew theirs—it was infuriating how many facts he'd managed to pick up in a few short minutes. Still, with any luck, he'd be on his way to the fast road by now, all set for the Hotel Voltaire at Lille. There might even *be* a Hotel Voltaire at Lille. Finding she had blundered into busy shopping streets, she told herself to concentrate.

'Est-ce que je peux avoir le clef de notre chambre?' Sian muttered from the back, practising with her French phrase-book.

Annabel tuned her out. She was on a fast out-of-town road, the last thing she wanted. She peered ahead for a helpful turning and, when it came, edged out of the one-way flow and back to streets ever more congested as they reached the centre. Rain thudded on the roof, the back windows, misted up, and the search for their hotel seemed to go on for hours.

'There's the Voltaire! Sian said at last.

And it was, away from the centre in a quiet, open street, with plenty of parking. They stopped as near as they could for the dash through the rain, and arrived in the lobby hand-in-hand, warmed by the exercise, with only heads and shoulders really soaked. Before approaching the desk, Annabel paused to run a hand through her daughter's rough hair, shaking the wet from the ends. Sian submitted, but her eyes continued wide and alert, greedy for as much of Abroad as they could take in.

'He's here, ' she presently announced with a satisfaction that struck her mother as downright sinister. 'I thought he might be, after what I told him.'

'Who?'

Annabel guessed the answer even as she turned to survey the long reception area. So this was why Sian had been content to hold her questions for a while. Caird was waiting for them, just springing up from a deep leather couch by the desk.

'You little . . . ' Annabel began through gritted teeth, and he was upon them.

'No Blythes expected,' he began cheerily, 'so I thought I'd wait, in case your booking's been snarled up.'

'We aren't called Blythe.' Sian's head tilted to one side in surprise. 'Where did you get that idea?'

'Oh, I don't know, people get funny ideas.' He ruffled her hair exactly as her mother had just done, inspected his wet fingers, and pulled a clean handkerchief from his pocket. 'If you'll just hold still a minute . . . '

He spread the handkerchief over her hair and rubbed, the very model of a caring father, while his eyes considered Annabel. She refused to meet them, refused any hint of an answer to the question in them. She had changed her name to escape her past, start a new life, and keep him off her track. Let him work that out for himself.

'No need to dry her here,' she told him curtly. 'There'll be towels in the room.'

'We're called Stroud, like the town in

Gloucester,' Sian piped from under the handkerchief. 'Oh,' she plucked it off to stare up at
him, 'your name's Gloster, isn't it?'

He thrust the handkerchief in his pocket. 'You
know me?'

'I didn't know you were my . . .' She paused,
looking from one to the other. 'I mean, I heard you
say . . .'

Her bewildered, uncertain expression made
Annabel forget all her embarrassment and her
anger with them both. Poor little love, she
thought, none of this is her fault. She pulled Sian
close to her side, and was rewarded with one of
those quick, trusting smiles which had always
made everything worth while.

However, her satisfaction was short-lived. Safe
under her sheltering arm, Sian felt able to pursue
her interest in Caird.

'I saw your programme about the poor little
ponies.'

'Ah, yes!' He had been staring at the two of
them, his eyes unreadable. Now he came to himself with a start. 'We had lots of letters after that
one, from little girls like you.'

'Hayley wrote,' she nodded, 'and you wrote
back—she showed off like anything about it. Wait
till I tell her . . . ' She stopped, worried again.
'What *do* I tell her, Mummy?'

'When we're in our room,' Annabel met Caird's
eyes with a signal which she saw he understood,
'we'll have a talk about it. But for now . . .'

She looked longingly through the glass door.
How much more comfortable it was out there, rain

and all, than in here with the troubles Caird had brought upon her. The damage was done though, the day of reckoning had come and she was forced at last to talk to Sian about her father. But first she was going to tell him what she thought of him, before it choked her.

'Sian,' she was careful to keep her voice level, 'do you remember how to ask for the key?'

'*Le clef.*' Sian's eyes grew enormous with delight. 'I'll go and get it, shall I?'

Annabel watched her hurry to the desk, then turned to Caird, tight-lipped. 'Why did you ask me where we were heading, when you'd already got it out of Sian?'

'She'd forgotten the name of the hotel. Besides, fool that I was,' his eyes hardened over something like despair, 'I was hoping to find I could trust you . . .'

'Trust me?' she repeated, outraged at the cool presumption that she owed him the truth or anything else. 'Do you think . . .'

'I didn't think anything. I just . . .' he looked over to Sian at the desk '. . . just hoped.'

She would have answered him, but was silenced by the unguarded pain and longing she had glimpsed briefly in his eyes. He wasn't going to give way to it, didn't want her to see it, but for a moment it wouldn't be hidden. She watched his averted face, saw him fighting for self-control and turned back to her with his usual calm.

'You know, Annabel, you still haven't given me a hearing.'

Now it was her turn to look away. If he didn't

want to show his feelings, why should she be
moved by them? But she couldn't help it. Had she
been wrong all these years, to keep Sian to herself?
She had always been proud of her determination
to manage on her own, but he was making her feel
her pride was wrong-headed and selfish. It wasn't
that he deserved any consideration from her, she
told herself, but maybe for Sian's sake she should
have got in touch with him. He'd certainly have
helped. After his divorce, he might even have
married her.

Which was ridiculous—he'd have made her
miserable. She'd been miserable anyway, but at
least lived on her terms, made her own way, and
come out of the experience a complete, independent human being. She faced him with
renewed strength.

'I don't owe you a thing, Caird Gloster.'

'Except your daughter.' He spoke gently, not
arguing but stating a fact, and the doubts started
up again. She'd been through this tangle so often,
especially in her early years of hardship. It would
have been so easy to wish she'd never set eyes on
him, and during her pregnancy she often had. But
never since. Never since, for how could she wish
away Sian? How could she even regret loving him,
when out of that love had come the chief joy of her
life?

'We've talked enough,' she began, and stopped.
She sounded almost pleading, and she wasn't
going to plead. Admit nothing and show no
weakness, that was the only way to handle this.

'You haven't talked, you know.' Still gentle, he

corrected her. 'All you've done is fence.'

'Sorry to disappoint you.'

'You're still fencing.'

'For goodness' sake, Caird!' She felt the exclamation torn out of her by his obstinate calm. 'What do you want?'

'Well, when I first saw you I wanted the chance to . . .' He stopped, glancing again to where Sian was standing on tiptoe now to run her finger down the hotel register. 'It doesn't matter,' he went on, still watching. 'That was before I knew. Now, I just want a chance to get acquainted with my daughter.' He dragged his eyes away from Sian and met Annabel's again. 'Is that so hard to understand?'

'I—I'd never expect it of you.'

'There's a lot you don't know about me,' he spoke lower and faster as Sian took the key and started back towards them, 'and a lot I want to know about both of you. Have dinner with me?'

She looked out throught the streaming glass. Another British car had just pulled up, the family within preparing for their dash through the rain.'We'll be eating here——' she began.

'Me, too. So we'd be silly not to eat together.'

She let out a quick sigh of exasperation, hounded into a corner as she pictured the absurdity of their eating at separate tables. 'All right,' she agreed reluctantly. 'If you'll . . . '

'Number Seven.' Sian had reached them waving the key with its heavy brass tag. 'He thought we hadn't booked at first. Then when he found our name, he called us Stroo . . .'

She tried to imitate the French way of saying their name, and went off into a shower of giggles. Caird joined in, suddenly full of high spirits—having got his own way as usual, Annabel thought sourly.

'What about your luggage?' he asked, still chuckling. 'Can I bring it in for you?'

'You haven't got the message, have you?' she burst out in irritation. 'We're a team, us Strouds. We organise ourselves.'

He sobered abruptly. She realised with surprise that she had wanted to show him where Sian really belonged, and, what was more, she'd succeeded. She'd drawn a circle round the Strouds with him outside it, and he knew it. Sian, too, had sensed the tension, and was staring from one to the other in bewilderment. He glanced down at her, and as if by conscious effort relaxed his manner and voice into easy persuasion.

'Somebody has to get soaked. I'd rather it was me.'

His self-control make her feel suddenly churlish. What was she trying to prove? Certainly she had been careful to pack all their overnight things in one small bag she could easily bring in herself, but why look for trouble in an ordinary, kindly offer of help? Why not accept it in the spirit it was made?

'All right.' In spite of her effort, she still sounded ungracious to her own ears. 'You can take Sian's keys.'

'Goody!' Sian brought the keys out of their special inner pocket. 'I'll come too, and open up . . .'

'Oh, no, you won't!' Annabel and Caird said together.

Annabel looked at him, abashed. He had spoken so exactly like herself, and with exactly the same determination to stop their daughter going out into the downpour. How strange to hear another person caring for Sian in so very much her own way, humorous and bossy, restraining and loving. She saw his quizzical glance and knew he, too, had been taken aback.

Sian was clapping. 'Link fingers!'

'Not now, darling.'

'But, Mummy, you spoke exactly together. You can't just throw your wish away like that.'

'What is all this?' Caird asked. 'What wish?'

Sian explained, 'When two people speak exactly together, they each get a wish. Only, they have to link little fingers before they wish it, and say a poet's name after.'

'I see. Like this?'

He held up his right hand. Annabel stood indecisive, then had her mind made up when Sian seized and joined their hands.

Don't be silly, she told herself, and braced her arm to stop the shivers spreading up it. She saw that her sleeve had dropped back, exposing the pulse in her wrist which throbbed her need of him like a teleprinter. The British family trooped in and she moved thankfully to let them pass, trying to draw her hand clear.

He closed his tight, keeping it prisoner. 'I haven't wished yet—have you?'

She shook her head, closed her eyes in despera-

tion, and in the coloured darkness behind her lids
sought a wish to free her from this invasion. That
Caird should go away and leave them alone? She
didn't even know if she wanted that any more.
She had been growing less sure of it by the
minute, and now with his hand warm against hers
she was almost certain she wanted nothing but to
keep him here at her side.

'Poet's name, Mummy.'

Annabel hastily wished for better weather.
'Shakespeare.'

'Robert Burns,' Caird said.

She opened her eyes, found his fixed on her
face, and cleared her throat. 'Give him your keys,
darling, and we'll go up to our room.'

Reluctant but resigned, Sian handed over her
precious keys. Annabel watched with relief, glad
to have her mind taken up with ordinary, everyday things again. Then, with a touch on her
daughter's shoulder, she turned them both to the
stairs.

But Caird wasn't done with her yet. Before she
could move away she felt his hand on her arm. It
was such a familiar hand. She knew its strength,
and how in spite of that strength it had never once
dealt her anything but tenderness. She had often
pondered that too, in the long, lonely nights,
wondering why she in her weakness had to be so
assertive, while he who could have taken anything
he wanted was so unfailingly gentle. Her bitter
conclusion was always the same: he could afford to
be. Life had been good to him in so many ways.
She pulled her arm against her body, and he sensed

her resistance at once. He let his hand drop away, while his other tossed the keys lightly and caught them.

'You haven't told me what I bring in?'

'Dark red grip on the back seat,' she snapped, and made her escape at last.

CHAPTER THREE

THE room was enormous and welcoming. The twin beds took up a mere corner of it, the partitioned-off bathroom another, and that still left the corner by the window for table, chairs, and a standard lamp which Sian rushed to switch on. She would have opened the floor-length window on to the tiny wrought-iron balcony, too, but Annabel stopped her in time. They seemed to be on the weather side of the building, and rain was surging against the glass like buckets being emptied.

Thwarted, Sian went into the bathroom. 'There's soap here, a dear little packet with ''Hotel Voltaire'' on it . . . Mummy! You're not going to use it, are you?'

'You can keep the wrapper.' Annabel undid it carefully. 'Do you want to stop me washing, after all I've been through?'

'Goodness, I never asked you! Were you really sick?'

'Like anything.'

'But . . . then . . . when did you find . . . my father? Was he being sick, too?'

'No.' Annabel looked at their two reflections in the glass. 'I suppose he's like you, doesn't get seasick.' She turned on the taps and splashed her face, conscious that the promised talk couldn't be put off much longer.

She had never lied to Sian about her origins, but

she had never told the whole truth, either.
Mummy had once loved a man very much, but the
man had gone away. No, he wouldn't be back.
No, his name didn't matter, it wouldn't mean anything—the evasions came back to haunt her. She
had always meant to tell the whole story one day.
When it stopped hurting. When the child was old
enough to understand. When Caird stopped
appearing in those programmes which were still so
high in the ratings.

'When I saw him on telly, I wondered,' Sian was
saying thoughtfully. 'It's funny when your father
could be anybody.'

Annabel groped for the towel, eyes smarting
and heart twisting with guilt. She knew exactly
how it felt to wonder if the postman, or your
teacher, or the man in the moon, was your father.
She should have said something long ago, given
the child something to hang on to, but . . . how?
And here came the questions.

'Why was he so cross with you, mummy?'

'He wasn't cross.' Annabel instinctively headed
her off that one. 'He . . . he likes you.'

'I like him, too. He's nice, isn't he?'

'I . . . I suppose so.'

'So why did he go away from us?'

'He . . .' Annabel stalled for time. 'It's a long
story . . .'

The firm double knock at the door, so like
everything Caird did, came almost as a relief. Sian
ran to open it, while Annabel tried to think of a
way of telling the story which wouldn't make it
sound too sordid. Bad enough that her daughter

should have to wait till she was nine years old to meet her father for the first time—the real truth about him would make it even worse. The child had just welcomed Caird into the room with the wet overnight bag, and was giving him a conducted tour while he shook rain out of his hair.

'And we've two chairs.' She pointed to them, all hostess. 'You can have that one, and Mummy can have this.'

'Thank you, madam.' Annabel approached them. 'But Caird has to go now . . '

'He can't go yet, Mummy.' The little chin squared up. 'He might be able to tell us.'

'Tell you what?' Caird looked from one to the other.

Sian planted herself in front of him, feet apart, hands behind her back. 'I was just asking Mummy why you left us.'

In the sudden quiet, rain lashing in renewed fury at the window, he was ominously still. 'What do you mean?'

Annabel moved to the overnight bag. 'I must unpack . . .'

'Sit down!'

She sat.

'Now,' he went on to Sian, 'tell me what you mean.'

Annabel felt suddenly helpless against the two of them—the tall man with hands in pockets, legs apart, the small girl facing him in exactly the same posture. They were so alike, and so determined to go on with their enquiries, she could do nothing now but wait for the outcome. She braced herself.

'Before I was born,' Sian explained, 'why did you go away?'

His hands came out of his pockets and balled into fists as he swung round to tower over Annabel, white-lipped. Then he dragged in a long breath and let it out slowly, hands unclenching, relaxing by an effort of will. The eyes he turned back on Sian were gently interested and teasing.

'I bet you couldn't order our drinks.'

'I bet I could!' She rose to the challenge at once. 'What do you want? I'll make them understand, you'll see.'

'Let's be going, then.'

But Sian hadn't finished with him yet. 'You like being my father, don't you?'

He nodded. 'Full marks, chicken. You're the nicest present I ever had.'

'So why did you go away . . .'

'We'll talk about that,' he shot Annabel a stormy glance, 'after we've eaten, maybe.'

'Are you going to be with us all evening, then?'

'You don't like the idea?' The pain showed in his eyes briefly, to be dispelled by her quick response.

'Of course I do. People ought to know their fathers, oughtn't they?'

'I'm glad you think that.' His smile was suddenly rich and invigorated. 'Let's go, then.'

'But . . . I don't know what to *call* you,' she sounded exasperated. 'Mr Gloster sounds silly, and Caird's all wrong . . .'

'So why not Dad?'

'No!' Annabel rapped out before she could stop herself. Two pairs of eyes levelled on her, and she added lamely, 'I . . . don't want that. You can make it . . . Father, if you like.'

Even that word, with all its overtones, stuck in her throat. Fathers ought to earn their titles, love their children and take care of them, not suddenly appear out of the blue and work their way in with professional charm. Resentment flowed through her and drew her to her feet—the sooner this unwanted evening was over, the better.

'Right, Father,' Sian said, and put her hand in Caird's.

They had their drinks in the long, narrow bar of the hotel. Its plate-glass wall gave a clear view of what should have been a cheerful, bustling street, but was at the moment a wet desert with teeming gutters and ever more rain leaping from the lowering sky. Indoors, however, the lights shone gold in their raffia shades, twinkled on the bottles and spread with a buttery sheen on the shiny black table-tops. Annabel asked for cognac. She didn't usually drink anything so strong, but then she didn't usually have the kind of day she'd just had. Caird chose whisky, and Sian climbed on a stool to give the orders while they waited on either side of her.

The street door opened to let in a wet gust of wind, a squelch of shoes on the lino, and a harsh voice which sounded unexpectedly close behind them. 'Well, well, if it isn't me old friend Caird Gloster!' The lantern-jawed speaker pulled off his cap to show fairish hair plastered lank to his head. 'How are you, Caird? Ruined any honest tradesmen lately?'

Caird turned slowly, met the hostile stare, and stepped forwards, as if to shield his companions with his broad back. 'I never bother honest men, Denny.'

'No? Funny. Thought that was all you did do.' The narrow head leant to one side, releasing a smell of unwashed damp hair as the small eyes flicked over Annabel and Sian. 'Having a few days off, then? Taking the wife and kids out of all the aggro?'

'No aggro, Denny. None at home and . . . none here?'

The last two words put a cool question and answered it, both at once. Caird stood in his favourite posture, feet apart, facing square on to any possible trouble. He looked relaxed and cool, but Annabel knew that the hands so casually thrust in his pockets were in reality poised there, ready to cope, ready to grab, ready to lash out if need be with all the force of the six-foot-three, fourteen-stone body he was balancing so lightly on the forward part of his feet.

The newcomer saw it, too, and the ferrety eyes came to their decision. 'Funny, I don't want a drink any more. Too particular about my company, I suppose.'

He settled the cloth cap back on his head, pulled the jacket up to his chin, and padded out. Caird looked after him with a frown which didn't clear after the man had disappeared from view along the windswept pavement beyond the plate-glass wall.

'I take it you exposed some racket he was running?' Annabel asked, impressed in spite of herself.

'Not Denny, he was never big enough.' Caird turned back to the bar, saw their drinks waiting, and pulled his wallet from an inner pocket. 'He was mixed up in some action we had over phoney language schools.'

'I heard that one at Hayley's,' Sian said. 'It was people paying to send their children abroad . . .'

'Right.' Caird took up his glass to warm between his hands. 'Only they never learnt languages. They washed dishes and scrubbed floors.'

'The man you interviewed talked a lot of bleeps, and smashed the tape recorder.'

'That wasn't Denny. But he was in there somewhere, helping.'

'I didn't like the way he looked at you.' Annabel shivered. She hadn't liked the way Denny looked at her and Sian, either.

Caird dismissed the incident. 'Drink up, and we'll eat.'

The restaurant was as inviting as the bar. Vases of sturdy marigolds glowed on every windowsill, and a long, central table held cheeseboards, cartwheels of pastry, and bowls piled high with summer fruit.

'I'm hungry.'

Sian sounded surprised, and Annabel knew exactly what she meant. The place was so full of spicy smells, such a riot of appetising colour, you'd feel hungry here even if you'd just eaten— which they hadn't. Her own lunch, she remembered, had been wasted, and the breakfast boiled egg seemed a long way off.

They started with quiche lorraine. Annabel tasted it carefully at first, wearing her professional hat. By the end of the first light, subtly flavoured mouthful, she was ready to admit the chef knew what he or she was doing, and settled down to enjoy herself. The chicken that followed was dressed with an egg and cream sauce which the menu called *vallée d'Auge*, and by the time it was finished only Sian had appetite left to sample the *quatre-quarts* cake. Annabel took one of the superb peaches from sheer greed, and Caird finished with a piece of camembert.

'They know how to buy their wine here, too.' He gestured to the empty brown pitcher which had held their order of house wine. 'Shall I ask for some more?'

Annabel shook her head. 'I'm sleepy enough already. And it's your bedtime, madam.'

'We're Abroad, Mummy.' Sian looked mutinous. 'I haven't seen it yet, 'cept through the car window.'

'And the rain,' her mother reminded her.

'We've got our macs.'

Annabel looked at the last watery daylight behind the bright flowers. A walk before bed might be a good idea at that—it would help all this food to settle. 'Right,' she said. 'If you'll excuse us, Caird . . .'

'Oh no, Mummy! Sian turned to Caird. 'You'll come, too, won't you, Father?'

What Sian called their macs were, in fact,

luminous tops and trousers, Sian's yellow and
Annabel's orange. When they rustled down to the
lobby, Caird looked them over with a smile.

'Sensible.'

'What about you?' Annabel glanced at his usual
leather jacket. 'You'll be soaked.'

'I've got my umbrella.' He showed it, hooked
over his arm. 'Do you know about the Burghers,
half-pint?

Sian nodded. 'We have those in England, too.
Only, I don't think I'm hungry any more, thank
you.'

'Hungry?' He puzzled for a moment, then
laughed. 'These Burghers aren't food, they're
history. There's a statue of them here I'm very
fond of.'

He put his umbrella and guided them along the
narrow pavement while he told the story of the
Burghers of Calais. Annabel kept behind, heavy
with food, hearing only the scraps that floated
back to her.

'. . . Edward the third . . . siege . . . citizens with
halters round their necks . . .'

She put up her hood and lost the rest. How a
good meal changed your outlook, she reflected as
she dodged an approaching umbrella. Two hours
ago she'd have hated this, trailing along in the
rain, having to watch the way Sian had taken to
her father. Now she didn't mind a bit; in fact, she
was enjoying the time to herself, without that little
voice clattering its endless questions. It made her
realise how busy she'd been in the past ten years.

Right from the start, she'd resolved that Sian's

childhood would be completely different from her own. She'd repeated her mother's pattern in falling pregnant so young, but from there on she would break out of it. No string of lovers for her, no long nights out while her daughter waited at home, lonely and afraid, no rave-ups like the one which had ended in that last drunken car-ride. Conscious of the need to keep Sian always in her mind, she had deliberately frozen out any man who approached. She knew she had sometimes caused offence, might even have harmed her business by it, but her catering skills, her reliability and her willingness to work had more than made up for that. She'd done well, and Sian had managed without a father.

Or had she? Look at her now, eagerly questioning, learning new ways of looking at the world, seeing everyday things from competely new angles—maybe, after all, Caird ought to have been allowed a part in her upbringing. That's being wise after the event, she answered herself stubbornly; I wasn't to know he'd react like this. But the other voice in her persisted, shouldn't you at least have tried to find out how he would react?

She pushed it away, concentrating instead on this dream holiday she was at last able to afford. For as long as she could remember, during all the desolate years before and after her mother died, she had followed *The Sound of Music* from one cinema to the next. Its colour and music had been her only refuge in those days, and she still thought of Salzburg as a magic city, waiting to spread its riches before her, if only she could reach it. And she *would* reach it, in spite of Caird. At supper, he had spoken of the farmhouse he'd bought, and Sian was obviously longing to go there instead, but it was in Upper Austria, much too far from Salzburg. No, in the morning he would go his way and they would go theirs, to the city of her dreams.

She enjoyed the Rodin, green-bronze and towering in its small park. Each of the six conquered Burghers was a believable person, different in age and character from the others, yet united with them in dignity under their humiliating rope halters. Annabel walked round it, taking in the grandness and the pathos.

'I always think it's as much street-theatre as sculpture,' Caird observed, pleased to see how much they liked it.

'Look,' Sian said, 'this one's only young . . .'

By the time they had finished studying it, darkness had fallen. Noticing Caird's umbrella, furled and hanging over his arm, Annabel put her hood back cautiously, and found the rain had stopped. They returned the same way they had come, with Sian delaying her bedtime at every shop window. Annabel tried walking on and leaving her, but only found herself waiting at a street corner while, a hundred yards back, her daughter studied a chemist's model of the human digestive system.

'She's interested in everything, isn't she?' Caird came up to the corner. 'She does you credit, Bel.'

She glanced at him sharply, but couldn't doubt his sincerity. He was staring at Sian with pride, pleasure, amused exasperation—all the emotions she had known in herself for so long

'I . . . I often wonderd what you'd think of her.' She fiddled with the zip at her throat, pulling it down to let the cool night air reach her skin. 'I . . . I'm glad you like her.'

'*Like* her . . .' He paused, frowning. 'Why did you tell her I deserted you?'

'It wasn't like that, Caird, honestly.'

'That's how it came across.' His face darkened as he remembered, but clearly the worst of his rage was over, soothed by good food and exercise., Nevertheless, he warned her, 'I won't lose you again, you know.'

She nodded, resigned. 'I suppose you'll want to visit her?'

'More than that . . .' The harsh streetlight cast angular shadows over the strong planes of his face. 'Much more.'

She stiffened. 'Just what have you in mind, then?'

'Having you both to stay. Showing her off . . .'

'She's not a performing poodle!'

' . . . to my parents,' he snapped, rebuking her hasty misunderstanding. 'It isn't just a father you've robbed her of all these years, it's two grandparents.'

'Grandparents!'

She caught her brerath, silenced by the new idea. Never having had grandparents of her own, she simply hadn't considered the possibility of any for Sian. She shook her head angrily, the crumpled plastic hood round her collar rustling in sympathy. This was becoming altogether too complicated. It wasn't for her to consider two people whose existence she hadn't until this moment been aware of. Sian was doing fine without grandparents—without Caird too, for that matter— he'd just said as much.

But the complications wouldn't go away just because she pretended they weren't there. They had started the minute he'd recognised his daughter—she realised with a shock how that moment had altered her whole life and, more important, Sian's. She had better come to terms with the fact that he was here to stay. And, after all, he'd be a good father. Loving, sensible, able as he had shown this evening to enrich the child's life in ways she would never have thought of. Why not make the most of him? It would be all right as long as she managed to stay in control, let him know it was she who defined the terms.

Only, how did you stay in control of a man whose every approach shattered your self-possession to fragments? Even now, she noticed that she had unconsciously edged away from him and huddled herself together, her body better aware than her busy, distracted mind of how important it was to avoid all contact with him. And how did you dictate terms to a man who was so clearly used to living on his own, running things his way?

Well, she'd just have to try. After all, she'd come a long way in ten years. Now was the time to test how far, and prove her hard-won independence to herself as well as to him.

'Right,' she began, and gathered courage from the firmness and decision in her voice, 'if you give us plenty of notice, I might let her stay with you. In school holidays . . .'

'And you?'

Stiffening her resolution, Annabel met his eyes and found them unreadable in the shadows cast by the streetlights. All the better. 'I'll have to come with her once. To . . .' she smiled inwardly at the point she was scoring, but kept her voice even ' . . . to make sure you know how to look after her.'

The night-shadows swooped down over his face again, but he was only nodding. 'I can see you'd be helpful there, explaining what she's used to.' Could it be bitterness, that new note in his voice? 'Kids need their routine, don't they? You can upset them if you have things too different from what they're used to.'

'They change so much,' she reminded him with a gentleness which surprised herself. 'They're having a hard enough time coping with that. So they want everything else to stay the same.'

The shadows on his face flew sideways now as he turned to face her. She looked down hastily. She still couldn't see his eyes but, even without that, a new and disturbing interest showed in the angle of his head, the set of his mouth. She was unprepared for his hand on her arm, and started away from him like a wary animal. She didn't dislodge his hand though; it held her arm captive even as she distanced the rest of herself. Thank goodness for the plastic skin of her cagoule protecting her from the liquefying warmth of his touch almost as efficiently as it had protected her earlier from the rain. Instead it was producing a welcome rustling coolness as he pressed it, still wet from the rain, against her skin.

'That's right, isn't it?' he was saying in a wondering tone. 'Why did I never think of that for myself?''

'You have to be around kids, that's all.' She dared to look at him, puzzled by the importance he was giving her casual comment. 'And you haven't much, have you?'

'Not with the kind of help you've just given me.'

The bitterness was back in his voice, not against her but against something in his own mind, some unknown force or event in his past that had left its mark on him. She remembered that brief glimpse she'd had on the boat of a pain that gnawed at him and made his discovery of Sian particularly poignant for some reason he wasn't talking about. She wondered what it was. Could he have fathered other children, perhaps, and lost them when his wife refused to put up with his unfaithfulness?

It seemed all too likely. He'd tried to tell her she'd changed his life. Brought me to a full stop, he'd said; made me take stock of myself. Too late for his marriage, she reflected, remembering a passing reference she had read in the paper to the fact that he was divorced. No wonder he was shrugging it off now, covering his feelings with movement and dropping his hand from her arm as if it might give too much away.

'You can have Sian to stay, seeing you're so keen,' she told him. 'But I've got a business to run . . .'

'A business?' He grabbed the subject as if glad of the distraction. 'Little Annabel Blythe, a businesswoman . . .'

'Not so little!' She drew herself to her full five foot six.

'Cooking, is it?'

'Outside catering, from home.' She rushed on, proud to fill in the details. 'I started in a small way—parties, weddings, that sort of thing—but now I supply hotels and freezer firms as well. When we moved to North Street, I fitted a kitchen with all the equipment, and now I have three paid helpers . . .'

'And it does smell yummy sometimes.' Sian came up to join them. 'And listen, did you know you have pipes inside you . . .'

Annabel laughed and took her hand, drawing her alongside and firmly forbidding any more shop windows. It was Caird's turn to walk behind, something malicious noted from the back of her mind, and besides, it wouldn't do him any harm to see how well she and Sian got on together. She was enjoying her daughter's high spirits all the more after the rest she'd had from them.

They were almost back to the hotel. They turned into a wider road, still active with cars that sped by amid pungent smells of French petrol. One of them, a red Renault, slowed down and nosed in to the pavement. Assuming the driver was going to ask the way, Annabel looked round for Caird. She found it odd to think of him being able to instruct a Frenchman on how to find the way in a French city, but he did seem to have a working knowledge of the place. And, after all, Calais proudly proclaimed itself the biggest passenger port in the country, so a lot of visitors must come here from other parts of France. The man in the passenger seat wasn't winding his window down but opening his door and getting out, perhaps to be absolutely sure he understood where he was to go next. He had a black woolly cap pulled down very low, keeping the rain off his face, presumably . . .

Everything started happening at once. Sian's hand was wrenched from her own as the child was snatched up; in another moment she would have been in the car, but Caird must have reacted like a fired bullet. Annabel never saw him hurtle from behind, he was just there. Something whizzed down and she realised it was the umbrella, landing on the assailant's shoulder with such force she thought she could hear bone crunching. An animal yelp of pain, a string of foul language, and Sian was free to rush back, tripping a little over something which had just landed on the pavement.

It was the black cap. Without its concealment, Danny's lank hair clung to his neck as he struggled back into the car, with Caird hanging on to one greasy sleeve. The car shot away with the door open, dragging Caird along with it until its speed pulled him off his feet and left him full-length on the wet pavement. He was up at once, staring after the speeding car, but by then it was already small in the distance.

CHAPTER FOUR

IT HAD all happened too fast to be afraid, let alone to scream. Feeling delayed-action shock starting in the pit of her stomach and spreading acid into her throat, Annabel gathered Sian in and would have held her tight, but the child wriggled away to peer up at her father.

'Are you all right?'

'What d'you mean, is *he* all right?' Annabel choked. 'What about you? You're the one they were trying to . . .'

'I'm fine, Mummy, you can see I am. Father . . .' She brushed at the scuffs on the leather jacket.

He scanned her with a frown that looked thunderous in the wan streetlight. 'Sure you're not hurt?'

She shook her head. 'Didn't you hit him hard!'

'Not hard enough. Come on, no time to lose.' He took her hand and hurried her in the direction of the Voltaire.

So once more Annabel was trailing behind them, and this time fuming more at every step. She shivered, hating to think of what had nearly happened. But she must, it might not be over yet. The would-be kidnappers had got away, who knew what they were planning next? The world had suddenly become a dirty, dangerous place, and it was all Caird's fault. It was bad enough that he had thrust his company on them in the first place, but to involve them in this! Denny had nothing against her and Sian, he'd never have come near them if they'd been on their own. It was Caird, insisting on his share of the fatherhood he'd done nothing to earn—scheming and tricking for it—who had made his daughter into a target for any small-time or big-time crook with a grudge against him. The sooner they could be rid of him, the better.

And yet, how would they manage now without him? What would she do if those villains followed her car tomorrow and made another attempt after she had shaken Caird off? For all her hatred of him, she had to admit it was he who had saved Sian. She squirmed in shame as she remembered her own frozen helplessness throughout the action—but for goodness' sake, you didn't come out for a holiday stroll prepared for violence! Or perhaps Caird did—he dealt with it all the time on his wretched programme.

They were almost at the hotel now, and stopping for Caird to pull something from under the windscreen wiper of a parked grey Mercedes. Tucking the grubby envelope in his pocket, he looked tense yet resigned, almost relieved. He opened the plate-glass door of the lobby for them, hushing Sian's eager questions and addressing the clerk in his own terse French.

Annabel drew in a breath to protests as he took both keys, but he frowned her to silence and shepherded them to the stairs with himself behind them. He made her feel surrounded, arms up and hands spread in watchful defence, while his bulk stayed between them and trouble. At their door she turned, about to demand her key, but found her throat had gone dry at his closeness. She could smell the warmed leather of his jacket, and under that a wilder scent, the scent of a roused and fighting male.

He wasn't surrounding them now, but pushing them gently to one side. 'Don't come in till I tell you,' he ordered as he opened the door and deliberately closed it behind him.

He was checking, of course. A determined ill-wisher could easily find a way into this first-floor room with balcony, and could hide once he was in. But who would ever have wished them ill if they hadn't met Caird? To make matters worse, Sian seemed to be thriving on the excitement, bright-eyed and pink-cheeked, as if she'd been given a special treat.

'Isn't he marvellous? she demanded, far gone in hero-worship. 'Aren't we lucky we've got him to look after us?'

Annabel drew a shuddering breath through her teeth. Where did she start? Before she could, the door re-opened and Caird was giving them permission to enter the room she herself had booked and would presently be paying for with her own money.

'When I've gone,' he said, 'lock the door.'

'Where are you going?' She was dismayed and furious at the fear which twisted in her at the idea of being without him.

'*Gendarmerie* . . . they're probably looking for the

little louse already, I might be able to help them . . . don't worry,' his preoccupied frown softened as he took in her expression, 'I'll be as quick as I can.'

She bristled. 'I'm not worried.'

'All right, but don't take liberties, either. I'll knock like this . . .' He beat a patterned, familiar tattoo on the door. 'Ask who it is, and don't open till you hear my voice. In you go, half-pint.' He ruffled Sian's hair and lingered, infinitely tender, to cup the back of the small head in his palm. 'And don't budge from there.'

Annabel pushed her daughter into the room and closed the door. With the sound of Caird's footsteps retreating down the corridor, she turned the key as he'd instructed, reminding herself that this was mere common sense, anyway.

'Right, madam.' Relieved at the way her voice kept its usual firmness, she began the process of undressing Sian, by pulling off her waterproof and hanging it to dry. 'Bed for you.'

'But, Mummy . . .' Sian was interrupted by a yawn. She fought it till her eyes watered and won, but when Annabel pointed to the bathroom she moved towards it without further protest.

Annabel took off her own cagoule, feeling horribly unprotected in her jeans and sleeveless top. 'I'll bring your pyjamas,' she called, working to make her voice calm and strong.

Sian's pyjamas were, in fact, a cotton T-shirt printed with a horse, plus any pair of briefs that happened to be handy. Long-legged and skimpy, she settled into her chosen bed.

'Father says I'm to have this one.'

'Does he, indeed?' Hearing the sharpness in her voice, Annabel forced herself to relax. She couldn't let herself take it out on the child. Besides, the bed nearer the wall and further from the window was obviously safer for her—again, it was simple common sense. But some time soon she was going to warn Sian against quoting her father in those adoring tones.

She switched on the lamp and handed over the book she had taken from her bag. *Jill's Midnight Pony* could be guaranteed to spellbind Sian for the short time needed to soothe and get her to sleep. Then she sat on the edge of the bed for a goodnight hug, holding the beloved little bird-bones against her breast, resting her cheek on the light-brown hair, inhaling the scent of hotel soap from the fine skin and trying her hardest not to think about what might have happened.

Sian leant back against her round bolster. 'I shall stay awake till Father comes back, and hug him goodnight, too.'

Annabel rose abruptly and walked to the window, but it was blanked by the shutters which Caird must have bolted together before he let them enter the room. The green-painted steel was louvred with metal slits to let the air through. They let in some streetlight too, filtering through in parallel lines like the bars of a cage. And, on the other side of those bars, under that streetlight, who knew what was waiting?

Desperate for distraction, she went back to the overnight bag and busied herself, setting out her own needs for the night ahead. She didn't intend to undress and go to bed, not tonight, but she could at least clean her teeth, brush her hair, wash her face. Seeing the maps sticking out of the back pocket of the bag, she seized them with relief. The mere act of spreading the big one on the table under the yellow light from the standard lamp heartened her and helped her to push her troubles into the back of her mind. This was their immediate future, this straight line through Lille and all of Belgium, past Cologne and Frankfurt and Nuremburg and Munich, one more frontier into Austria and there it would be, Salzburg in all its splendour. Not knowing how fast she could travel or by which route, she hadn't booked any more rooms, and now she was glad of it. She was going to move that Polo for all it was worth—by mid-morning tomorrow she'd have left Caird and Calais, Denny and all his works far behind. Would she take this route along the Rhine, or this one through the vineyards of the Mosel? She sat down to compare them, and the soft, rhythmic knock had sounded twice before she heard it.

It had always been their secret signal, that rhythm of *Rule Britannia* tapped out with just the cushions of the fingers. As she stood up, the memories flooded back before she could stop them. So many times she'd knocked on his door like that. She mustn't, mustn't think of what had always come after her knock; it had nothing to do with anything. But it wasn't fear now that prickled her bare arms with goose-flesh as she went back to the door.

She called out, heard his answering voice, let him in, and got away as quickly as she could. Sian was drooping sideways, fast asleep but still propped almost upright in her determination to stay awake until her father got back.

'Put the top light off,' Annabel murmured over her shoulder.

He obeyed, and the white overhead glare went out. By the softness of the bedside light, she eased the warm little body down between the sheets. Sian gave a huge sigh and settled on her side facing the wall. She went on breathing deeply and evenly as Annabel pulled the covers round her, picked up the horse book from the floor, and put it on their shared bedside table. She hesitated a moment, then switched off the bedside lamp, leaving a soft darkness tempered only by the distant gold of the standard lamp in the far corner of the room.

'Spark out,' Caird whispered. He had come to the other side of Sian's bed, and now stooped to kiss a pink ear that showed between the silky strands of hair.

Annabel pulled her arms against her body and hugged her elbows. She couldn't deny the love in that gesture—yet how could he feel so deeply for a daughter he'd only discovered today? He didn't know her, had never gone through any of the day-by-day routine which made a real parent-child relationship—or anyway, not with Sian.

'You must have other children?' she asked resentfully.

'Only one. A girl.'

He was looking away from her, but even his profile showed a bitterness she was beginning to recognise. It was in the angle of his head, the clenching jaw, the tightening lines round his mouth. To her horror, she wanted to comfort him, to draw him into her arms and kiss the pain from those haunted eyes. She started away from the temptation, walking as lightly as she could on the creaking boards to the softly lit table where the maps were waiting to be folded. The quiet activity soothed her again, and she was able to reflect that, after all, if he'd lost his daughter it was his own fault. He should have taken better care of his marriage.

'I suppose your wife got custody.' She made it a statement rather than a question.

'Leave it, Bel.' Caird took the chair nearer the window, and lowered the dark briefcase he had been carrying. 'It's a tricky subject.'

'I'll bet!' So he wanted Sian to fill the gap, her child, who was his by the merest accident of conception.

He had left the briefcase now and was facing her, hard-eyed. 'I thought we'd at least got over this bit, Bel.'

'I don't know what you . . .'

'For God's sake!'

He had spoken too loud, his fist thudding the table. Annabel instinctively looked to the further of the two beds, but Sian hadn't stirred. The six o'clock start and the excitements of the day had caught up with her, and the only movement under

the covers was the quiet rise and fall of her
breathing.
'this fencing!' Caird went on in a hissing whisper.
'We've just been through a pretty nasty experience . . .'

'And whose fault was that?'

He leant forward, hands clutching the edges of
the table. 'Are you going to sit there and pass
judgement, or do you want to hear what I've been
finding out?'

'You've learnt something?' Her agitation was
back, hammering in her throat. 'How?'

'At my car, for a start.'

She nodded. With so much else to worry her,
she had completely forgotten the envelope he had
taken from the grey car. 'Was that a message from
them?'

'I had to leave it with the police,' he raised his
briefcase and riffled throught it, 'but they let me
have a copy.'

He pushed it across to her, a photocopy of a
twisted scrawl wandering mindlessly upward at
the end of each line, without heading or signature:

'If you want to see her again put all your stuff
abt Gull Cove in a envelop & post to . . .' a London
box number followed, printed in block capitals
' . . . when it gets their you can have her back, if it
is not their in seven days you mite get an ear or a
toe . . .' Annabel dropped it, feeling sick.

'It didn't happen.' Caird reminded her, 'and it
won't.'

'You seem very sure.'

'I am.' He pointed to the marks near the top of

the paper, 'Trust Denny to leave his thumbprint.'

Not touching the horrible thing, she peered at it more closely. One of the marks was indeed a thumbprint, smeared but with enough of it clear to incriminate. She looked a wordless question.

'I was able to tell them where he hangs out,' Caird confirmed. 'They're looking for him now.'

'Does that mean we'll have to wait here and identify him?' Her stomach curled at the idea of having to see again the writer of that letter.

'If they get him' he agreed doubtfully. 'I wouldn't expect him to sit down and wait to be caught, though.'

'Great.' She walked to the window, then turned her back on it so as not to look at the barred shutters. 'He's still loose, and you're telling me I've nothing to worry about.'

'I didn't say that.'

He, too, stood up, hands out. She put hers hastily behind her back, in case he wanted to take them, but he only spread his own wide apart at that same guard-keeping angle, and once more she had the feeling of being surrounded, protected, comforted. Yes, comforted, she had to admit it. With this wall of bone and sinew and watchful brain between them and danger, she could already feel herself less tense, the knot of fear in her stomach beginning to unwind itself.

But that only drove her all the harder at her second worry. What was she going to do about this trembling awareness spreading through every part of her? It was less tumultuous now, but that only made it all the more overpowering. The still air of this room had suddenly become a bubble of time on its own, so different from everyday life that anything could happen here. The occasional drone of late evening traffic from the street, the occasional hotel-sound from the corridor only served to emphasise the quiet. And, in that quiet, she could no longer deny her longing for his hands on her flesh, for the smoothness of his skin against her fingers, for all the velvety hills and hollows of pleasure they had explored together so long ago.

So long ago, and nothing since. It had been easy to keep men away from her all this time, because she hadn't wanted them, hadn't even thought about them much in the midst of her endless chores. And now those years of busy emptiness came back at her like a long starvation, demanding at last to be fed. She could feel the need blossoming deep inside her—worse, could tell he recognised it and was meeting it with a need of his own. In the filtered light he was all in shadow, but the knowledge came to her in his stillness, the sudden change in the rhythm of his breathing, the softening curve of his hands as they moved closer to her and lingered an inch from her arms. The message leapt the narrow gap from his flesh to hers, spread its loosening warmth to her shoulders, her neck, her breasts, her nipples that had sprung to attention and now thrust their twin demands through the restraint of her bra and the loose cotton of her blouse.

This must stop! She huddled herself together, clutched her elbows again, turned away from the light. 'So what are you telling me, then?'

'Only that I'm with you and staying with you,' he murmured. 'Nothing's going to shift me till I know you're both safe.'

'But Caird, our being with you is why it happened!'

'I know, love, and if I could go back and change that . . .'

He sighed and turned away from her to look at the bed in the corner. Annabel followed his gaze to where the small, sleeping head was just visible in the dimness, and found she was breathing more easily. Concentrating on Sian and her safety was like reaching high ground in a flood; if she could only stay there, these longings that still washed about her could be ignored, might perhaps even subside and leave her in peace.

'But it's done,' he was going on briskly, 'so we've got to think about what's best with things as they are.'

She couldn't help responding to his authority. He must have dealt with so much trouble in his time, so much evil and so many of the people who brought it about. She waited.

'He's an odd one, Denny. Bilingual in French, fluent in Italian and German, gets by in Spanish . . .'

'I don't want a list of his qualifications!' she burst out.

He hardened his voice in rebuke, and went on, 'Anybody else would've hopped on a boat to Dover by now. Not Denny. He could take off in any direction.'

'I see.' She felt suddenly cold. 'Including ours.'

'Could be. The fastest way out of town takes you straight to Belgium, and Belgian and German motorways are free.'

She nodded. 'So if he's hard up . . .'

'Not only that. It means the only controls he has to worry about are at the frontiers. And an old hand like Denny knows how to deal with those.'

'How's that?' she asked, remembering the queues at the docks for Customs and passport control.

He shrugged. 'Couldn't be easier. You simply cross by minor roads. On some of them, the border hardly exists.'

'So he could already be ahead of us somewhere.'

'Worse than could, I'm afraid,' he told her gently. 'Salzburg's one of the places he operates. He knows it well.'

'My God!' She thrust his arm aside and walked past him in a passion of resentment at what he'd let them in for. 'A fine holiday this is turning out to be.' She stood at the table and tossed her head irritably as she felt his presence by her. 'Get away from me. I wish I'd never set eyes on you.

'You don't, you know,' He kept his voice a soothing murmur as he moved back to his chair. 'Now, turn off the fireworks and try a bit of thinking.'

She riffled through the maps on the table, dropped them, and turned her back on him. 'And where would that get me?'

'Why, Pankl's, of course. My farm,' he answered her next question before she could put it, 'miles away from Salzburg, by the Czech frontier. The nearest town's twenty miles off . . .'

'And you expect me to be pleased about that?'

'Sian will be.'

'Oh, you . . .'

She stopped, baffled by his cool certainty and by the simple fact that he was right. She remembered his chat over supper of the woods and meadows round Pankl's, the old house with its views down to the village, the rebuilding and renovations supervised for him by an Austrian architect friend. Sian was already spellbound by his account of squirrels playing in the larches near the house, the white goats kept by the neighbouring farmer, the wild ducklings on the river; but when he mentioned the riding-stables in the village she had cast imploring looks at her mother. It had needed all Annabel's carefully cultivated hardness to hold off the unspoken invitation hovering over them at that moment.

Now it looked as if she must accept it and be grateful. 'Just when I was hoping to get her interested in something other than horses,' she exclaimed in exasperation.

He grinned. 'In a fortnight?'

Annabel had to smile ruefully. 'Well, at least I could have given her something else to think about for a change.'

'She's already got that.' He glanced to the bed in the corner. 'As I have. How could you, Bel?'

She dropped the map and leant on the table, suddenly exhausted. Had she really made such an enormous mistake? Had she really, by hiding from him, been depriving all of them? Losing them a relationship that would have been valuable to all three? She sank to the chair opposite him and braced her hands against the table.

'What would you have done if I'd told you?'

'Why, married you, of course,' he answered promptly.

'How could you do that? You were married already.'

So that's what you thought?' He stared at her, and sighed. 'Isn't it just like you, to get an idea in your head . . .'

'But . . . she signed the register as . . .' Annabel paused, taking in what he was telling her. 'Then . . . you *weren't* . . .?'

'The divorce came through six months before we met.' Something in the memory was tightening his mouth, etching those lines of suffering again round his eyes. 'Millie kept my name because it suited her professionally—her research work was well known by then.'

'Research work?'

'She's a micro-biologist. A good one—that was part of the trouble.'

She scarcely heard him, back as he was in a past they hadn't shared. So they could have married. She had thought of being married to him, dreamt of it sometimes, especially in those first few years as a poorly paid employee at the King's Arms. The dreams had become less frequent as she grew busier, having more and more work put on her. Finally, when she'd wakened to the fact she was practically running the place and might as well be making all this effort on her own behalf, they had almost ceased. Now she was too proud of her hard-won success ever to think of giving it up. And she'd been better without him, she told herself fiercely, making her own life, working against the odds and achieving a business that was respected everywhere in the town.

'I wouldn't have taken you,' she told him, 'and, if I had, it wouldn't have worked.'

He leant back with a sigh. 'There you go. Bel has spoken.'

'Well, would it?' she demanded, nettled at the reminder that he considered her a know-all. 'Your other one didn't, however much you loved your daughter . . .'

'Careful.'

She glanced across at him, startled anew by the the steel in his voice. He was sitting upright again, stiff-lipped against the pain he couldn't quite conceal.

'We'd better get this straight now, Bel. We don't talk about my other daughter. Right?'

She eyed him, half inclined to challenge this cool instruction about what she might or might not discuss. One glance at the set features changed her mind; she already knew better than to argue with Caird in this mood. Seeing he had made his point, he gave a small nod, bent to his briefcase, and set on the table a litre of whisky with the red duty-free label.

'Now don't pull that face, you need something.' He followed the bottle with two minute tumblers, poured a small measure into each, and went past her to the bathroom. When he returned he was carrying a plastic mug full of water. 'Say when?'

'To the top. Do you always carry two glasses with you?'

'You'd be surprised,' he gave her a glance from under his eyebrows, 'how often they come in useful.'

'I doubt if I would.'

'There you go again.' He took his place opposite her. 'You won't be told, will you?'

She wrinkled her nose and sipped. The whisky was smoother than she expected, with overtones of peat and heather. She could almost enjoy it, and it was certainly making her feel better—stronger, and at the same time more relaxed. Caird was taking his without water, warming the glass between his hands and enjoying the smell. When he spoke, he sounded resigned.

'I suppose I'll have to keep telling you.' He put the glass down and leant forward to capture her eyes with his own. 'I don't sleep around. I never did. Got that?'

She sipped again, and found with surprise the tiny glass was empty. Yes, and she felt fine, ready for anything. It was true her eyelids were heavy, but she could still smile at him through her lashes, still let her fingers wander across the table, seemingly of their own accord, and brush the back of his hand. And when he turned his hand over, palm-to-palm with hers, his fingers moving softly against the flesh of her wrist, she could cope with that, too. It didn't mean anything, this singing in her blood, this stillness in her head, this demanding emptiness inside her. She didn't love him, no, she didn't . . .

'Oh, Annabel!'

He sounded almost scolding, yet when he stood up he retained her hand, captured the other, pulled her up beside him. She came to him willingly, close, close, until his arms were all round her, pressing her nipples against the leather of his jacket, pressing her thighs against the hot fullness of his loins. She put her hand up to caress that dear square jaw, and realised she had been wanting to do this ever since she first saw him. It felt a little rough, just as it always had this time of night, just as his neck had always presented this firm, muscled surface, and his hair this smooth compliance to her questing fingers.

The kiss was like coming home and wondering why you ever left. As long as these arms were round her, she was safe. These hard lips might be seeking out and savouring hers, this great male creature might want her, but he would take care of her, too—he always had. She let her lips part for him to taste the moist inner curves of hers, sent her tongue to enjoy the steadiness of his exploring mouth, closed her eyes and prepared to let him do whatever he wanted.

Caird drew away and looked down at her, mouth a little open, brows a little raised. She couldn't read his expresssion, so she closed her eyes again, and felt his gentle tug at the bow fastening the neck of her blouse. It parted, the air was cool at the base of her throat and then his lips moved against the exact place the bow had been covering. Her whole body, every inch of her,

everywhere, clamoured for the sensations he
knew so well how to arouse. Then he raised his
head, took her by the shoulders, and held her
away from him.

'There's unfinished business between you and
me, love.'

'Unfinished business,' she repeated drowsily,
and her eyes snapped open. 'What am I doing?
With Sian asleep over there! We must be mad!'

His right hand relaxed its grip on her shoulder
to smooth its way up her neck, part her hair at
the nape, cup the back of her head in much the
same gesture she'd seen earlier when he touched
Sian. She stiffened.

'You'd better go.'

'No, love.'

She jerked away from him, terrified of his
caresses, knowing how little she could resist
them. 'You must!'

'No.'

She glared at him, and realise he was much
calmer than she, even had a hint of a smile.

'What I *must* do,' he went on, 'is stay here.'

'Caird . . .'

'Steady, love! He reached out to touch her
again, then changed his mind and deliberately
held back. 'What d'you take me for? D'you
really think I'd want it here, like this . . .'

'Then go, for goodness' sake!'

'No,' he shook his head emphatically. 'My
room's on the floor above. I can't look after you
from there.'

Almost unconsciously, she found herself relaxing, her tense muscles loosening and fatigue taking over. If he was going to look after them, they'd be all right.

'But . . . how will you sleep?' She glanced round the sparse furnishings. There wasn't even a carpet, let alone an easy chair where he might spend the night.

'I'll manage.' He opened the wardrobe, and came over to her with his arms full of bedding. 'You'd better get some sleep.'

She nodded, and took her severe cotton pyjamas from the bag. When she emerged from the bathroom, carefully not looking at him, and slid into the unoccupied bed, she was amazed how comfortably it received her.

Caird had already arranged his own makeshift bed by the window. 'Good night, my love,' he said as he put out the light. In the darkness, she heard him quietly settling between the blankets, and then somehow it was morning.

CHAPTER FIVE

IT WAS Caird folding back the shutters which wakened her. A cloudy grey light seeped through the net curtains, showing his blankets neatly stacked and his pillows dumped on Sian's bed. Sian herself was invisible, but rushing watery noises came from the other side of the closed bathroom door.

'I showed her how to use the shower,' Caird explained. For one who had spent the night on the floor, he looked remarkably organised and fresh, though his shirt was open at the neck and his hair hung in damp tendrils. 'I showered too, before you woke—I hope that's all right?'

Annabel sat up and yawned, not bothering to answer. How typical of Caird to do what he wanted and ask about it later! Not that she would have thought of refusing him a shower, but it just showed how he went his own way and only pretended to be considerate about it.

'Now you're awake,' he added, 'I'm going up to my room to change my shirt. Lock the door after me, will you?'

There he went, giving orders as usual. She flung aside the sheet and swung her feet to the floor as her quickening brain suddenly presented her with a detailed picture of last night's events. Had that really been herself, so carried away she had wanted to . . . her mind veered off what she had wanted, but she couldn't stop the colour rising to her cheeks as she crossed the room. To make matters worse, the cotton of her pyjamas was brushing against her in featherlight caresses, the shadows of those she had longed for last night, and her disturbed, unsatisfied senses were responding with wave after wave of desire that washed into her brain and slowed her thinking. She glanced down at her breasts and, yes, her nipples were giving her away again, straining against their covering and broadcasting their demands to any who cared to read them. She tried her favourite trick of huddling herself together, but that only pushed her breasts into a different shape which made problems more conspicuous. She dropped her arms hastily and looked everywhere but at Caird.

But of course that was no use, she had to steal a glance to see if he'd noticed. He was standing with one hand on the knob of the door, the other about to turn the key beneath it. Both hands relaxed and fell to his sides as his eyes and mind clearly busied themselves elsewhere.

'To quote our daughter,' his voice came out rough and deep in his throat, 'yummy.'

The only way to cope with this, she decided, was head-on. Accordingly, she drew herself up and looked straight into the hazel eyes that were appraising her with such open enjoyment. 'Is that supposed to be flattering?'

'You do more for those pyjamas . . .'

Conscious of his eyes still on the twin peaks,

she cut in desperately, 'I wouldn't know.'

'Blushing, too! Annabel Blythe, you really are something.'

'For goodness' sake, Caird, go if you're going, and don't keep me standing here.'

'Sorry, love.' He turned away. 'It was quite an evening. Denny's got a lot to answer for . . .'

The mention of that seedy crook somehow completed her humiliation. He'd written that foul note, yet for a while she'd forgotten it, and him, too, forgotten everything and let her starved senses take over. It mustn't happen again.

To her relief, Caird was unlocking the door at last. 'I'll just bring my stuff down here, and then I'm done with my room.'

'I suppose you're going to pay for it? she asked, glad to apply her mind to something neutral.

'Of course.'

'It seems a waste, when you didn't use it.'

'These things happen.'

He let himself out and she turned the key with relief. She was almost grateful to him for the reminder of the way he lived. Yes, to him these things certainly happened; he would frequently find himself paying for one bed and then spending a causal night in another. She must hold that in the front of her mind during the days ahead.

Caird returned with a surprising amount of luggage. He seemed to have taken all sorts of odd things up to his room last night—a toolbag, a typewriter, a medium-sized suitcase and a shiny cylindrical duffel-bag. He met her questioning look with a grin.

'Let's have breakfast, then I'll explain.'

They breakfasted in the bar, still yellow-lit against the greyness on the other side of the plate-glass window, and scented now with coffee and fresh bread and fruity apricot jam. Their croissants were smoking from the oven, and flaked at a touch.

'Finished?' Caird asked, and put down the bowl-shaped cup which had held his own coffee. Brisk and matter of fact, he went on, 'I wanted breakfast inside us before I told you this. They've vandalised my car.'

Annabel had been wiping her fingers on her paper serviette. She dropped it and folded her hands on her lap instead, the better to control them. Luckily, she didn't have to speak, Sian was asking all the questions. The tyres had been slashed, the lock forced, the fascia worked loose, presumably with a crowbar, the instruments damaged beyond repair. An attempt had been made on the boot as well, but the lock there had held.

'I expect they were interrupted,' Caird said. 'So at least I've got my luggage.'

'They weren't ordinary thieves, then.' Annabel spoke for the first time since hearing the news, slowly and carefully to hide the sick tremor in her voice. 'Or they'd have gone for your luggage first.'

'Not ordinary thieves, no.'

He was pinching the bridge of his nose, moulding it between finger and thumb as if to persuade it back to its original shape. She hadn't seen him do that before, but then, it hadn't been broken when she last knew him. She supposed it had been done by another of his many enemies, and shivered at the thought of the trouble he must have stirred up for himself over the years.

'What was that place called?' This, she found, was the nearest she could come to speaking of the note he had shown her last night. 'Gull Cove, wasn't it?'

'It's an area of outstanding natural beauty,' he told her, 'and now somebody's trying to build a multi-storey hotel there.'

'How did you get involved?' Though of course she knew—that damned programme.

'It's to have discos, amusement arcades, a bowling alley—they ought never to have got planning permission.'

'I see.' She brushed the breakfast crumbs into a heap, grateful for the everyday smoothness of the plastic tabletop, the ordinary grittiness of the bits that stuck to the side of her hand. 'Corruption?' and when he nodded again, 'But where does . . . Denny . . . come in?

'I don't know, love. Maybe somebody's paying him, maybe he fancies a spot of blackmail.'

'Papers. He asked you for papers.'

'Dynamite,' Caird confirmed. 'They're with the bank.'

Sian had tried to follow the discussion and given up. 'Sorry about your car, Father. What're you going to do?'

'I got it hauled away last night, half-pint.'
Though he was answering Sian, his eyes were
holding Annabel's. 'Seeing it'll take days to fix,
I'm travelling in yours.'

'I'm only insured for one driver,' Annabel said
quickly.

'So drive.'

It was something, anyway, to see Sian so
pleased. When she heard they were going to the
farm after all, she turned bright pink and was
silent for a whole five minutes, taking it in.

The clerk this morning was a slim, dark
woman, her olive good looks enhanced by make-
up and a dress that managed to be elegant,
businesslike and seductive all at once. When
they returned their keys, she eyed Caird with an
interest which reminded Annabel what an
attractive man he was. That cool competence,
those powerful, athletic movements, those
steady hazel eyes would make any woman look
twice. However, this time at least, he wasn't
reading the message, or was ignoring it.

He stowed his luggage with surprising ease in
the boot of the Polo, all but the suitcase. That
ended up on the back seat next to Sian, who
claimed it added to her comfort by giving her
something to rest against. Following Caird's
clear directions about which road to take,
Annabel got them out of town quickly, in spite of
the busy morning traffic.

She was conscious of a huge relief as they
gathered speed on the fast road through French

Flanders. Partly it was because they were on their way, with Calais and the incidents of last night behind them. But equally it was her discovery that, while she kept her mind on the tricky business of negotiating French traffic, she could resist Caird's dominating presence in the front passenger seat, and her own crazy thoughts about how it would be to have him with them like this for good. For good? The very word was a mockery, she told herself, and concentrated on her driving.

He hardly spoke until Lille, and then it was to give directions which took them through it as neatly as he had taken them out of Calais. Only as they left it behind, with the traffic thinning again into countryside, did he make a brief, wry comment on the lie she had told him yesterday.

'It's famous for its Hotel Voltaire, Lille.'

She ignored him easily enough with the frontier ahead and passports to be shown. To Sian's disgust, nobody at the frontier took any notice of them, and the first few minutes in Belgium were loud with her complaints.

'Let's have coffee at the next stopping-place,' Caird said presently.

'No, I want to get on.' Annabel kept her eyes on the road. 'Besides, I've no Belgian money.'

'I have. But if you like we can just pull into a lay-by for your break.'

'My break?'

'You're over your two hours.'

'Oh, that.' She overtook a double-loader full of cars. 'You don't take that seriously, do you?'

'I certainly do.' He didn't sound annoyed, just cool and firm. 'On long journeys, you take five minutes off every two hours. Seeing you're the only driver . . .'

'Seeing I'm the driver, I'll decide when to stop.'

She sensed him turning to the back seat. 'How about you, half-pint? Do you want to stretch your legs?'

'Mummy,' Sian sounded a little worried, 'We're in a new country. You are going to let us walk about a bit, aren't you?'

They stopped at the next lay-by, and walked about a bit.

One more uneventful frontier brought them to Germany, where Caird won the argument about lunch, too. Annabel wanted to make the obvious stop at a motorway restaurant; he pointed out gently that in August these were seriously over-crowded. And so it turned out; she could barely find parking space, and every table in the restaurant was taken. Admitting defeat, she allowed him to guide her to a village with an unpronounceable name, where they ate excellent salads in a cool, cosy inn which enchanted Sian by the variety of the ice-creams it was offering.

The coffee was excellent too, but in spite of it Caird fell into a light sleep when they started moving again. Perhaps he hadn't done so well after all, on the floor with his blankets. So at least she could choose her own route, Annabel thought, and decided on the direct Cologne to

Frankfurt road. Only it didn't turn out like that; she must have missed her exit, and by the time she had got them out of the terrifying traffic round Cologne, they seemed to be heading for a place called Siegen. It was all right though, the next signs featured Frankfurt again, so they couldn't be that far off course. When Caird woke, she was able to pretend she had meant to come this way.

'Good,' he said. 'This is the route I like best.'

'We crossed the Rhine,' Sian piped up from the back. 'And Mummy swore at a man in a big car.'

Caird grinned. 'It *is* a bit hair-raising round Cologne.'

'I wasn't . . .' Annabel began and had to attend to her driving again, overtaking a lorry and a light van while a Porsche appeared out of nowhere and flashed its headlights impatiently.

'The motorways here have no speed limit,' Caird said as the Porsche sped by and vanished in the distance. 'And Frankfurt's terrible—the traffic just goes on and on.'

Annabel's heart sank. 'Worse than Cologne?'

'Much worse. How wise of you to pick this route, so we needn't go near it.'

'Mummy gets everything right,' Sian said happily.

Bless you, my love, Annabel thought, and felt some of her strain easing away. She could even smile at her own absurdity. If Caird had told her to come this way, she'd certainly have given him an argument; instead, she'd got here by bungling.

Even on this grey day it was a pretty road, its surface so good it was like being airborne, soaring over green valleys, where white-walled villages shone from miles away. The hills were wooded, with intriguing pathways crossing meadows and disappearing under trees. The prosperous, endlessly rolling countryside had little in the way of dramatic crags or castles or waterfalls, but Annabel found its quietness relaxing her from the stresses of the last twenty-four hours and the overpowering consciousness of Caird at her side.

'Any of these villages will have a good inn,' he said at about five. 'Shall we go looking?'

Her instinct was to keep driving, to put more miles between them and Calais, but she knew it was sheer blind panic and ought to be resisted. Accordingly they took the next exit, which led them to a quiet road unhedged between ploughed fields. A turn off this again and they were in a neat village square, a steepled church on one side and two ancient inns on the other.

Sian chose the Sonne because she liked its half-timbering. Caird booked the rooms, rattling off his request before Annabel could find any of the careful phrases she had been studying all winter. She listened to her daughter's admiring comments with a certain sourness, and hoped she would have some chance to practise her own German before her holiday was over.

The Sonne seemed to have taken centuries to settle into its present shape. Every immensely

thick wall had its own individual lines, but the
timbers were iron-hard and the floorboards
didn't utter a single creak. The peppery scent of
the windowbox geraniums drifted in through the
open windows, which on this side all looked
across the street to the church. In the wide
spaces of the room Sian rushed about exploring
and announced that the huge bed was really two
beds with separate mattresses and everything,
that the wardrobes smelt of cloves, and that the
shower . . . worked.

'Oh, well.' Annabel surveyed the small figure
with its hair and shoulders dripping wet. 'You
needed to change that T-shirt anyway. Give it
here and I'll wash it.'

Sian hauled it over her head, and Annabel put it
in the wash-basin. On second thoughts, she added
yesterday's discarded underwear and her own
blouse, which she changed for a navy long-sleeved
shirt that made her feel better protected. She had
run water into the basin and begun soaping when
Sian, hair towelled dry and wearing her clean
T-shirt, voiced her indignation.

'Mummy! A whole new country, and you're
washing!'

Annabel sighed. She could so well understand
the feelings of a lively nine-year-old, cooped up
in the car all day and now longing to explore. On
the other hand, the washing had to be done as
quickly as possible, to give it a chance to dry.

'I'll be as quick as I can, poppet. Couldn't you
just . . .'

Caird's *Rule Britannia* knock interrupted her,

and the problem was solved. First there was his room to be inspected—a single on the floor above, he told them, with a view out to the hills. When he had brought Sian back from that, he announced he wanted a newspaper, and appoached the wash-basin where Annabel was doggedly rinsing.

'You've been driving all day. You need to switch off for ten minutes.'

'Do I look tired, then? She watched the water drain away, and hoped he hadn't noticed the sudden anxiety in her tone. It had come out before she could stop it, and to her own ears was too revealing. Why should I want to look my best for him? she asked herself angrily, and jammed the plug back in place.

'Come on, love,' he laid a hand on her shoulder, 'put your feet up, and half-pint can come with me'

She turned on the cold tap hard and let it flow over her wrists. It didn't help though, her pulses were fluttering worse than ever, her whole consciousness rushing to that warm, gentle hand on her shoulder and raying out from it again in a languorous web of desire that held her paralysed. She ought to shrug it off, move away from him, think about something sensible. She was furious with herself for just standing here like this—yet, when he assumed her agreement and turned away to take care of Sian, life was suddenly colder, darker, emptier than it had been for ten years.

Left alone in the room, she finished the

washing and draped it over the towel rails.
When she moved to the window to look over the
square, Caird and Sian were just coming out of
the little Spar shop beyond the church. Sian held
the newspaper and was peering down at it with
such interest that Annabel wondered if she had
found a picture of a horse. Or maybe she was
just determined to have a go at understanding
the language—that would be very like her.
Anyway, she had given it to Caird, and he had it
tucked under his arm. The pair of them were
strolling away from the hotel now, Sian ahead
like an impatient puppy, then halting at some
command and waiting for him to catch up. She
took his hand and they moved together with that
familar long-legged stride, to the corner and out
of sight.

Annabel turned back into the room with a
miserable feeling of being left out. They got on
so well, those two. She might as well face it now
and decide what to do about it, though every
course of action seemed equally unattractive.

To stay with Caird in London was unthinkable
now. She would never have an easy moment,
wondering where his enemies would strike next.
It wouldn't be just for Sian she'd be worrying,
but for Caird himself—however much he
annoyed her, however much she wished he
would leave her alone, she found she couldn't
bear the thought of his being hurt. How on earth
did he stand this job which put him in danger
even on holiday, miles from home? No wonder
he'd bought a retreat half-way across Europe—

he needed it.

She pushed back the folded duvet on her half of the great bed, slipped off her shoes, and settled, with her feet up, to concentrate. Where, she wondered with her eyes on the restfully blank ceiling, did his parents live? Sian's grandparents—that too was something to think about. He seemed very sure, more than sure, that they'd want to know about her. Annabel's conscience dodged that one; she still found it hard to face the fact that her pride had come between Sian and all the loving attention grandparents might have been giving her. She would never have thought of Caird as a family man, yet here he was, taking on the role of father with such enthusiam and determination that she knew she would have to come to terms with him and let him into their lives somewhere.

The question was, where? And how? They could have him to stay in their own home, they had the space, but she hated to think of what his presence would do to her peace of mind. And whatever happened she must not, *must* not get involved with him again: once was enough. She felt the colour rise once more to her face as she remembered her reaction to him last night. He'd made no secret of finding her attractive, but then he wouldn't—she was sure the world was full of women Caird found attractive. No doubt many of them, like herself, carried the scars to prove it.

And that was it, wasn't it? If she wasn't careful, she was going to be hurt all over again, and hurt worse because she was older. She'd thought

herself safe, would have gone on thinking so if
Caird hadn't turned up and shown her how
fragile it was, this shell she had so carefully
constructed round her world.

He seemed so genuine, that was the trouble.
And he hadn't after all been married—that, too,
was a new thought to struggle with. No, he
hadn't been married—but his ex-wife had been
making herself at home in his room, *their* room
. . . her thoughts veered away from the pain of
the memory.

Well, he'd been right about one thing, she'd
needed this time alone to think things out. With all
the methodical thoroughness which had made
such a success of her business dealings, she
checked again through the problems she had been
considering and the conclusions she had reached.

Item: Sian now had a father in her life and
Caird a daughter in his. Item: Sian at least had a
right to the relationship and must have the
chance to develop it. Problem: this couldn't be
done in London and she didn't want him in
Rybridge. Possible solution: those grandparents—she must find out more about them.
Item: being with Caird bothered her, and the
way things were turning out she was having to
be with him too much. Item: she couldn't think
about him so much when she was busy; having
something that needed all her attention, as her
driving had done today, was a big help.
Solution: keep busy, have plenty to occupy her
while he was around, and avoid being alone
with him.

It was only a matter of planning ahead. She might, for instance, be unpacking the overnight bag now, but instead she would save it for later, and use it to fill a time that might otherwise be dangerous. And what about those letters she'd hoped to draft, one to her accountant and one to the couple who hadn't paid their bill yet? Not to mention that birthday party estimate, and the report she had to write for the Tech on this term's City and Guilds apprentice . . . she settled on her side, immensely soothed, and the next thing she knew Sian was shaking her awake.

'Great news, Mummy. They've got him.'

'Uh? Got who?' Annabel turned on her back for a luxurious stretch—it really was a very comfortable bed—and stopped in mid-yawn when she saw Caird standing a little further off, with a smile she didn't like at all. Not that he looked in the least aroused, as he'd been this morning, but somehow this fondness was worse, this pleasure in just having her there and looking at her, as if he had the right to take an interest in her. That was it, he'd established his right to behave as a father, and now he was looking at her like a . . . husband. A fond husband, glad to have given her a break and pleased to find her rested.

She sat up quickly. 'Stand back, will you?' She addressed both of them impartially while scanning the floor for her shoes. 'How can I get up while you're hemming me in like this?'

'You are *slow*. Mummy!' Sian stepped back as she'd been told, but didn't conceal her impatience.

'They've got Denny!'

'What?' Feet into shoes, Annabel sat up straight as her daughter could have wished. 'Who have?'

'The French police,' Caird said. 'Come on down, let's eat while we tell you about it.'

Light-headed with relief, she allowed them to guide her down the stairs to the beamed dining-room. Everything was marvellous—the scents of wood and wax and flowers, the big tables with their cushioned, high-backed benches, the heavy figured cloths and leather-covered menus and tiny vases of paper-frilled posies.

'Spices!' Sian had followed her keen young nose to the vase on their chosen table.

Sure enough, the flowers weren't flowers at all, but cloves, cinnamon, carraway, all lovingly assembled into flower shapes and interspersed with tiny fir-cones. Taking her turn to sniff, Annabel identified a vanilla pod formed into petals, poppy and mustard seeds thickly clustered round some kind of berry, and a piece of ginger wired to a stalk.

'What a super idea. We'll have to see if we can do some of these . . .' She broke off, realising that in her new sense of well-being she'd completely forgotten to ask for details. 'Come on then,' she put the vase back in its place, 'how did they get him? And how do you know?'

'Father telephoned from a special international call-box. He knows ever such a lot, Mummy . . .'

'You phoned the French police?' Annabel looked across at Caird, glad of the breadth of yellow and white tablecloth she had managed to put between them and of the subdued lighting which might hide the fact that she, too, was impressed.

He nodded. 'They were expecting to hear from me. And they got him this morning in St Omer. Driving a stolen car.'

She accepted the heavy menu and watched the waitress lighting their candle. 'So we needn't have been in such a rush.'

'Oh yes we did, Mummy,' Sian corrected her. 'How else are we going to have any time at Pankl's?'

'But . . .' Annabel put down the menu to let her whirling thoughts settle into their new patterns. 'We don't have to hide at the farm any longer. We can go to Salzburg.'

She didn't need to ask what Sian thought of that idea. The wide hazel eyes were at first incredulous, then frowning, and at last settled to a resolute glint which, like the straight mouth and clenched jaw, was all too familiar. When Sian was frustrated as badly as this she didn't bother with tears or tantrums, but simply showed her disapproval and went on showing it. She could keep it up for days. And a fine holiday that would make—Sian's holiday too, Annabel reminded herself; her daughter had a right to some choice, quite apart from the question of what to do with Caird now. They didn't need his protection any more, but he had set off with them and was relying on the transport to his farm.

Besides, he'd been useful as navigator, and helpful with Sian. It had been bliss just now to rest and know that someone else, someone interested and reliable, was taking over for a while. Yes, there were plenty of reasons for staying with him, quite apart from the feeling which hung at the edge of her mind and got in the way of all her clear, logical arguments. It wouldn't go away, but she needn't admit, even to herself, that she had . . . got used to the idea of a fortnight with Caird. That somehow Salzburg, without him, had lost some of its glitter.

She pushed that one aside and prepared to deal with Sian. Nine years of living with such a strong-willed little girl had taught her that these fits of temper must never be ignored. For Sian's own sake, they had to be acknowledged and worked through. Teaching her she didn't automatically get her own way all the time was part of helping her grow into a civilised human being. She drew a breath to speak, but Caird got there first.

'Come on, half-pint, less of the sulks.' His voice was teasing, but with an undertone of firmness, his mouth so like Sian's it was quite clear where she'd inherited her determination. 'Your mother's doing all the work, she has to make the choices.'

Amazement kept Annabel silent. Was he really talking Sian out of going to the farm, in spite of wanting so much to see her there? But no, this wasn't about where they went, it was about how

Sian behaved. He was simply doing his share of keeping her in order, and that alone was extraordinary enough. He might adore her, defend her, amuse her, but he wasn't going to be one of those fathers who enjoyed spoiling their children and left the discipline to the other partner.

Annabel was conscious of a huge relief. During these lonely years, the loneliest times of all had been when Sian was naughty. Then more than at any other time she had longed for someone to talk to, someone to back her or show her where she'd gone wrong, another viewpoint to help them sort themselves out. And now Caird of all people was helping with the burden she'd had to bear on her own for nine years.

'I never said a word,' Sian countered as Annabel had known she would; it was one of her favourite gambits.

'You didn't need to.' He murmured something to the waitress and began again when she departed. 'It's written all over you—you're going to be a right pain till you get your own way.'

Annabel blinked. What he said was true, of course, but to put it so brutally . . .

'Rotten old *Sound of Music*.' Sian was proving him right with every word. 'I never liked it, anyway.'

'But your mother does,' he persisted gently. 'And you never know, you might enjoy being where it was made.'

'Shan't. I'll hate it!'

'You're being silly.' The steel in Caird's voice

was nearer the surface. 'You'll miss a lot if you carry on like that.'

'But, Father, your farm! I was going to ride the horses . . .'

'And how d'you know there aren't any horses in Salzburg?'

'Are there?' Sian was brought to a halt by the idea.

'See? You don't know anything about it.'

Annabel couldn't help smiling. She had so often used those very words, but never with such devastating effect. His neat, concrete example had brought the argument right home, shown the child at once how little she understood.

Sian, however, didn't give up easily. 'I know *you* won't be there . . .'

'No, you don't,' he answered smartly. 'I'm coming with you.'

'What?' Annabel glared at him, 'Since when?'

'Since finding it's safe, of course—I couldn't have let you go near it before. Now, here's what we're going to do . . .'

The plan he outlined seemed sensible enough; they were to use Pankl's as a base. 'It's not all that easy to find places to stay in August, specially round Salzburg.'

'But your farm's miles from there——' Annabel began in outraged protest.

'With the motorway, a day's outing.'

'I don't want just a day's outing,' she told him furiously.

'But Mummy,' Sian chimed in, 'you're always

telling me we can't have everything we want.'

So they were back to the old line-up. Two pairs of eyes regarded her with the same reasonable demand; two busy minds worked to make her feel selfish, as well as silly, to be raising objections. She would have loved to bang their heads together. She picked up the menu and opened it.

'I'll take you as far as your farm,' she announced grimly. 'And then we'll see.'

CHAPTER SIX

IN SPITE of Annabel's reservations, supper was a high-spirited affair. Caird invited them to share a dish shown on the menus a *Hirtenspiess*, and Sian laughed herself silly at his unintentional pun when he translated it as 'Shepherd's spit'. It turned out to be what Annabel knew as kebabs: pieces of pork and bacon, with the occasional mushroom and onion ring, all on wooden skewers, lusciously grilled and perfectly set off by a herb-seasoned salad. With it came a silver platter of chips, so plentiful that Sian didn't leave herself room for any ice-cream. She still studied the illustrated ice-cream card, and asked if she might look at it again when they came back from their walk.

The dark was coming early again this evening, the wet grey light seeping away already and leaving a hint of rain behind it. It didn't matter though, the air smelt of grass and leaves and peace, and when Sian lingered they could sit on the bench by the church and wait for her, not worrying. Just not worrying, that by itself was enough to make Annabel light-headed, let alone her consciousness of Caird here at her side. He shifted to put his arm easily along the bench at her back, and it was good to be so surrounded, so protected, so warmed and sheltered by him.

Relaxing from the pressures of driving, drowsy with food and relief, she could have slept there and then, head on his shoulder.

And a lot of good that would do her. She sat up sharply and reminded herself that this relief was only the other side of the trouble he had caused by his very presence. And he'd got his own way again, making her go along with him, like it or not; he was, in fact, generally acting as if he were in charge and responsible for them. Well, he wasn't; it was *she* who ran her life and Sian's, yes, and she had made a good job of it, too, this far. She moved a little sideways, knowing that any contact with him, even the accidental brush of his fingers, would set her pulses racing.

'It's the last thing I'd ever have imagined about you.' She spoke more aggressively than she meant to. 'That you'd be so keen on being a father.'

'I keep telling you,' he placidly responded, 'there's a lot you don't know about me.'

Remembering the micro-biologist wife, the daughter he'd forbidden her to mention, she had to agree. How odd to think of another little girl somewhere who was Sian's half-sister. Did she too take after her father? Did she miss him? Did he see her much? She longed to ask, but his grim tone last night was still fresh in her mind. Right, if she couldn't speak of his marriage she'd at least hint at it.

'There always was,' she told him drily.

The remark hung in the air between them. Last

night he'd have picked it up and flung it back at
her, found a taunt to deliver in return, told
her—she remembered it with a distant indignation—that she was being a know-all again.
Now he only turned his head slowly, his eyes
reflective. She felt suddenly uncomfortable and
small, a bad-tempered Pekinese trying to pick a
fight with a Labrador.

'I've been thinking about all that, love.'

'You mean about . . .' she sought for the right
phrase, and couldn't find it '. . . about our
affair?'

He winced. Clearly, he too disliked the cheap
little word, with its casual, almost cynical overtones. And yet, what else was she to call it?
Whatever it had meant to her, an affair was what
it had been to him, so casual he hadn't even
bothered to keep his ex-wife out of it.

'You know——' he might have been reading her
thoughts '—it was more than that, for both of us.'

She stared ahead, defeated by his gentleness.
Sian had just picked up a kitten with the same
gentleness, supporting it with both hands, letting
it nestle on her shoulder, offering it whatever
caresses it chose to accept. Annabel suddenly
realised she had never really left Caird behind at
all. So much of him lived in their daughter, she'd
been unwittingly learning about him for years. The
athletic grace, the stubborn tenacity, the eager
inquisitiveness, all were qualities she knew well
from Sian, as she did this sensitive kindness
towards the weak and defenceless. For weak and
defenceless was exactly what she was, she saw

with blinding clarity, compared to this man beside her.

And she knew her daughter was genuine, straightforward, loyal—so perhaps Caird was, too. Maybe she ought to listen when he told her he'd never been as casual about sex as she believed. Perhaps his promiscuity really had been mostly in her mind.

'You said on the boat,' she began carefully, 'that I was a—a turning-point for you. Can you . . . tell me what that means?'

He shrugged. 'A lot happened to me about then. None of it good.'

'You got your own programme . . .'

'And lost . . . well, among other things, I lost you.'

'And that . . . mattered to you?'

She hardly dared to believe it, yet why not? Perhaps he meant it. And if it was true, if he'd really missed her, longed for her, sought her—why, then, she could at last admit her own longing, look steadily into the empty place in her own life, and acknowledge the need for him that had never, never left her.

'It wasn't the only thing.' He too was looking at Sian, the ache of loss clear in his eyes. 'Maybe it wasn't even the worst. But it mattered, yes.'

How could it be anything but honest, this painful evaluation of what she had meant to him? He wasn't speaking to flatter, but digging away at the facts as his professional training had taught him, hoping to come up with the truth for both of them. And yet, the truth had so many layers to it.

'How much . . .' She moved her head to indicate Sian. 'How much has it to do with her . . . your being sorry I left you?'

'Why nothing, love.' He seemed surprised at the question. 'I'm very, very glad she exists, but I didn't know about her at all till yesterday, remember?'

'Yet . . . you still minded?'

When he finally answered, his voice was low, its power banked down as he looked into the past and sought for words to show her what it had meant to him. 'We . . . didn't exactly part friends, did we? And that was sad, because . . .' his eyes met hers with difficult directness '. . . while we were together, you made me feel good. Very good indeed, Annabel Blythe.'

'I wasn't . . .' Her own voice came to her, puny and persistent like a demanding child's, yet she had to know. 'I wasn't just another fond memory, then?'

'You weren't a fond memory at all.' He smiled, his mouth quirking. 'You were a little pest, a little witch, you got right under my skin . . .' The smile faded, leaving a hungry intensity in its place. 'You made the sun come out.'

'You never said . . .'

'I wouldn't believe it. It took Millie . . .'

'Millie. Why was she there, Caird? In our room? When you felt as you say you did about me?'

'Wasn't it a mess?' The hunger settled to a weary sadness. 'She'd just turned up. Had to see me in a hurry, couldn't get a room, was sure I wouldn't mind sharing . . .'

'But that was *our* room . . .'

'I know, love,' he stared into the distance, 'I was trying to tell her, and it wasn't easy when I hadn't . . .' he turned back to Annabel, drinking her in '. . . hadn't admitted what you meant to me. The trouble was,' he sighed, the pain there again in his eyes, 'in spite of the divorce, she was hoping . . .'

'So I . . . finished off your marriage? she asked in a small voice, disliking this picture of herself as the other woman.

'No,' he shook his head vigorously. 'Things would only have been worse in . . .'

'In what, Caird?'

'Never mind, love.' He covered her hand with his own. 'Some day soon I'll tell you all that.'

She let it go, fearful of spoiling with stupid questions the new understanding which was growing between them. Knowing how much pain she had given him already by her insistence on talking of that time, she put her other hand over his. Perhaps, in the 'some day soon' he was promising, he would be able to share it with her.

They circled the village in dreamy content, planning for the next day. Caird said they wouldn't need another hotel; an early start, a long day's drive, and they could be at Pankl's tomorrow. Was Annabel game? Sian didn't speak, but her shiny sideways glance at her mother said it all. Annabel was game.

'Hello,' Caird indicated the sleek BMW parked by Neddy, 'more foreigners. That's an export number-plate.'

'Is it?' Annabel couldn't work up much interest. 'Come on tiddler, bed.'

This evening, the ritual protests were quickly settled. All it needed was to ask Sian if she really wanted to make Pankl's by tomorrow, and she forgot even her ice-cream. Caird tucked her up and claimed the first cuddle, while Annabel unpacked the overnight bag and remembered all the paperwork she had meant to do. She must at least complete the estimate, she thought with a sigh, and accepted Caird's offer to bring up her document folder while she kissed Sian goodnight.

While *Jill's Midnight Pony* worked its usual magic, Annabel drifted to the open window. The damp freshness of the evening filtered, geranium-scented, through the windowbox, and the church clock struck nine. On the pavement below, Caird stood hands in pockets, her folder under his arm, staring down at Neddy. Beside him was a girl who looked as Annabel, in her old revenge fantasies, had always dreamed of looking. Blonde hair shone opalescent in the streetlight, curving to smooth shoulders only half covered by a lacy wrap; small, perfect features were no doubt enhanced by skilful make-up, but you couldn't see the skill, only that the skin seemed flawless and the eyes enormous.

'I just think they're so cute, these little cars,' an American voice floated up to the window. 'They ought to wind up with great big keys.'

She's talking about Neddy, Annabel thought indignantly, annoyed with Caird for not putting the creature in her place. But then, he wouldn't, would he? Not anybody really, he was far too good-natured, and certainly not a woman who looked like this. She too was holding something, a big volume which might have been a road atlas. She must have taken it out of her car; the door of the BMW was still open. Yes, it *was* a road atlas, and Caird was asking if he might look through it.

'Why, sure.' The blonde fluttered lashes that had to be fake. 'Maybe you could help me find the way to Dubrovnik?'

They disappeared into the entrance, still talking, and Annabel turned abruptly from the window. She was surpised to find her lower lip caught between her teeth, and let it go with a long, outward breath. It felt bruised and tender, as if she had been biting down on it without knowing, and even now she realised suddenly that her teeth were clenched much too tight. She deliberately let her jaw relax, deliberately slowed herself down as she crossed again to the sleeping Sian, closed the book and slid the child further under the duvet. Sian heaved her usual sigh and moved on to her side; she was away for the night. Calmed as always by the contact with her sleeping daughter, Annabel cleared the table of the clutter that had accumulatd there, got out her pen, and sat down to wait for Caird to bring her papers.

He wasn't long, but when she let him in a whole new scent entered with him. Nothing in it recalled the country air they had just been enjoying; it was heavy with sandalwood and roses, and a muskiness which reminded Annabel of exclusive parties where she had been kept strictly in her place as caterer. That perfume cost as much as would support her and Sian for a month, and its expensiveness wafted round Caird as he held up her folder.

He sniffed, and grinned. 'Did you hear me talking to the American? She's playing in the Dubrovnik festival.'

'Playing . . .?'

'She's a pianist. Hungarian descent, studies in New York.'

Annabel managed a shaky laugh. 'You seem to have heard a lot about her in a minute or two.'

'That's show-business.' He smiled as if sharing a joke, and went on, 'Lend me that big map of yours a minute?'

She fetched it without a word. She couldn't have spoken; too many painful questions were jostling in her mind, taking all her attention and leaving nothing over for the simple, everyday comments she ought to have been making.

'She's called Teresa Something-or-other,' he went on. 'I'm to call her Tess.'

'And will you?' She handed him the map.

He smiled again, as if he didn't need to answer. 'She wants to go by Füssen, and see that castle of mad Ludwig's.'

'But wasn't that a road atlas she was holding?'

'You saw her?' He met her eyes with—could it be amusement? 'You'll understand the problem, then.'

She shook her head, bewildered. Could he

really be telling her, of all people, that this Teresa Something-or-other had made a dead set at him? Could he really be laughing about that, and expecting her to laugh, too?

'She has trouble where the pages join,' he explained. 'If I show her the route all spread out, no joins, she might have a chance of getting there.' He raised the map in cheerful salute. 'Are you going to be long?'

Again she shook her head, not trusting herself to speak.

'Good. I'll be right with you, then.'

It sounded reassuring enough. After his departure, she found she could assemble the figures she needed and get to work with her calculator, safe in the confidence his voice and manner had passed on to her, sure he would be back again before too long.

Not that she'd be able to talk to him when he did come back, not till she'd got this job out of the way. She ploughed on, estimating for the birthday cake she would make herself, adding in the cost of the salmon already in her freezer, looking up the price the wholesalers had quoted for eggs and oil to make the mayonnaise. Then there was the letter to write, in her best clear hand since she hadn't brought a typewriter. But, wait a minute, Caird had one. It would be much more businesslike to type the letter if she could—but not tonight, the noise would wake Sian. So that was that for this evening.

She stretched, consulted her watch, blinked, and looked at it more closely. Could it really be half-past ten? Why hadn't she heard the church clock? If it chimed ten strokes, it must have gone on and on—had she really been so busy she'd never noticed? She went to the window and looked at the lit-up dial. The minute hand stood exactly on the half-hour, jumping on as she watched, but she didn't hear a sound. Maybe the chimes were silenced at night—she must ask Caird if that was common practice here.

But where *was* Caird? He hadn't said how long he'd be, only that he'd soon be back.

Annabel felt suddenly cold. The freshness of the night washed over her with the green scent of geraniums, and she remembered that other, composite fragrance Caird had brought in with him—an hour and a half ago. That was how long he'd stayed with this Teresa Something, in spite of all his reassuring talk.

Free of the need to concentrate on the job, her daughter safe asleep, Annabel considered again the ways a woman's perfume could be left on a man. That creature must have been rubbing against him like a cat. He'd treated her as a joke, but then he would—when it came right down to it, he didn't take any woman seriously. No wonder his marriage had broken up. Women to him were something outside of everyday life, to be enjoyed and humoured in the interludes before he returned to that man's world of violence and double-dealing which had so horrified her in Calais.

The memory of last night, of that kiss and what might have come after, twisted in her like a knife. It had been hard enough for her, breaking that off;

it must have been worse for him. He wouldn't be used to such denials, and if a pretty woman made a dead set at a him when he had nothing to do . . . she shuddered and closed her eyes. When she opened them, she was ready to face the unpleasant facts. In the strange life he led, he must often meet women like this Teresa. Old habit died hard, and the frustration of last night had been just the extra push he needed. They must be together, comfortable and secret, with no little girl to hamper their lovemaking . . .

And to think that only this evening he'd talked about how much she'd meant to him. She had even begun to trust him. What a fool she'd been, when it only took this—this passing offer—to prove he would never change.

Quarter to eleven. They must be having a great time. Annabel was aware of pain in her hands, and realised when she raised them that it was her nails digging into her palms. She didn't unlock her fists at once, but stretched them at arm's length and circled them ahead of her to work off some of her tension. Then at last she was able to spread out her fingers and look at her square, work-worn hands, still rigid at shoulder-level in front of her eyes.

Dropping them to her side, she knew what was troubling her most. Not the feeling of being let down—she'd been through all that before, was almost expecting it this time. No, it was pure jealousy eating her now. The thought of Caird in bed with that beautiful woman was simply not to be borne. How dared he?

She'd show them. She knew his room number;

if they weren't there, she'd bang on every door till she found the woman's room, which was the only other place they could be. She'd wake the whole place up, embarrass the hell out of him, make him pay any way she could, she decided as she stalked along the corridor.

And in the morning, her fantasies flew on as she climbed the stairs, in the morning she'd drive off and leave him. Let him hitch a lift with his new lady, and see if he could persuade her to his wretched farm. Of course, there would be trouble with Sian, but that could be dealt with—must be dealt with, for how could Sian be allowed to go on idolising a father who could behave like this? It would have been much better if the child had never known him at all but, seeing that it couldn't be changed, the less they saw of each other the better.

She banged on Caird's door with all the force of an arm grown strong with hard work. They didn't answer; if they were in there, they must be waiting for her to go away. She banged again, and rattled the door-handle for good measure. It turned easily, and the door opened.

She smelt the perfume again, and heard small breathing sounds. As her eyes grew accustomed to the darkness, she made out a shape against the paleness of the bed, lit only by the streetlight filtering in at the window. They might at least have drawn the curtains! Her hand sought the light switch; let them be really shown up, and see if they had any shame.

It wasn't the ceiling light which responded but

the striplight over the washbasin. In its creamy glow, Caird slept on, stretched on the folded duvet, cheek burrowed into the pillow exactly like . . . exactly like Sian. He was quite alone, and as she took in details she didn't see how he could ever have had anyone with him. Nothing about him spoke of abandonment to passion, only to sleep. He was fully dressed, even to his shoes and leather jacket, the map she had lent him concertinaed on the floor where he had dropped it. He must have been sitting on the edge of the bed studying it, planning tomorrow's route, perhaps, and then decided he might as well relax for a minute while he waited for her to finish her estimate.

His too-long hair lay tangled over his eyes. His chest moved up and down in a steady rhythm and something about his helplessness, his total surrender to oblivion, went straight to her heart. After all, she'd known how tired he was—hadn't he already dropped off once today? And that was because, for Sian's sake and hers, he'd spent last night on hard wooden boards. He hadn't complained, just let her sleep, got up early and showered, taken the day easily and met her own aggressive contrariness with endless good humour.

And how had she repaid him? With bad temper, rudeness, suspicion, a willingness to believe the worst—she looked down at the fleecy rug, across to the little table with its one chair, anywhere but at the man she had been so quick to condemn. How could she ever think he'd do such a thing, right under her nose, after all his considerate kindness?

She recognised that kindness now. It was the very thing which had drawn her to him ten years ago. Yes, and it was his kindness which had responded to her, kindness to a lonely young girl burdened with the needs of a starved, unhappy childhood.

Why, even his success in radio and television had been based on kindness, a desire to help. People who were nothing to him, complete strangers, had been let down and left with nowhere to turn, so they had turned to Caird and he had done what he could for them. As he had for another stranger two hours ago, who had asked him the way. And because the stranger happened to be a glamorous woman, and because he hadn't reported back on time, Annabel had woven a whole snarled web of imagining round the two of them.

A know-all, he'd called her, and he'd been right. She'd jumped to conclusions, thought she knew it all, discounted everything he'd been trying to tell and to show her ever since this journey began. And now, looking down at his deep, defenceless sleep, she learnt something about herself which was worse.

She still hadn't grown up. If she'd really been so sure of herself, really been the sensible independent woman she wanted appear, she wouldn't have been so eager to impress him with her maturity. It would have shown anyway, and he would have recognised it. But she couldn't be mature with him, because she wasn't. That was why she had blamed him for the encounter with

Denny, when he'd suffered from it more than she had. That was why she had believed he could casually pick up a complete stranger, just to pass the two hours she couldn't be with him. This was how little she'd changed from the ignorant, lonely eighteen-year-old who, because she wanted so much to be with him, had lied about being protected from pregnancy and been caught by her own lie.

Being pregnant was her own fault as much as his. It was the first time she had ever admitted that, and now she had, she was going to be different. She would think less about herself, more about him, and for a start would do what she could to leave him comfortable for the night's sleep he so badly needed. She tiptoed to draw the curtains, then knelt by the bed and unlaced his shoes. He rolled on his back as she got them off, and another wave of the insistent perfume billowed over her—but she wasn't going down the road again. He was here alone and asleep, with all his clothes on, that was enough for her. His jacket was rucked under him now, she really ought to get him out of it before she left. She was trying to slide her hand under him when he stirred again, and wrinkled his eyes against the light.

'Don't, Millie, love. I'll be all right.'

Millie again. His wife must have meant a lot to him once. Whatever had parted them, it couldn't have been easy for him—but the marriage was over, past reviving, he'd been very clear about that only this evening.

So we might have been together all this time,

Annabel thought, I might have had a father for my child and the only man I've ever wanted for my husband . . . but she was letting herself be carried away. That was how things had turned out, let them be for the moment. He was moving again, putting out a hand, touching her cheek. She turned to press her lips against his fingers.

'Stop that!' He snatched his hand away and shot upright. 'My God, Teresa! Have I got to draw you a picture . . .'

'Hush, it's me.' Annabel sat on the bed and pushed the hair away from his face. 'If you don't want to be invaded while you're asleep, you'd better lock your door.'

He relaxed and smiled, a little awkward. 'Who do I think I am, anyway, Casanova?'

'She managed to get her perfume all over you,' Annabel pointed out gently. She wasn't accusing or asking how it happened, only reminding him he had reason to think the girl was attracted to him.

He smiled again, more comfortably now. 'She did wrap herself round me a bit.'

'And you didn't like it?'

With the best will in the world, she couldn't help a certain amount of disbelief. But the noise he made through his teeth, the lift of his brows as he turned to meet her eyes, showed only deep distaste—deeper, perhaps, than he cared to express.

'She only had one interest—herself. Maybe when I was younger I'd have put up with it . . .'

'She was so beautiful.'

'Packaging, love. Luckily, another guy turned up . . .'

'Another guest?'

He shook his head.' 'Outdoor type—he's up the road at the camp-site. I left them having dinner together.'

'And if he hadn't . . .' she broke off to giggle, but managed to finish '. . . hadn't rescued you?'

He looked awkward again. 'I thought of getting you down to scare her off . . .'

She threw her head back and laughed, to think of him needing her help against a pretty woman. 'Didn't you fancy her the least little bit, then?'

'You know who I fancy, Annabel Blythe.'

'But why didn't you come back upstairs like you said you would?' She spoke quickly, to distract herself from the hungry eyes which glowed directly into hers.

'I was going to . . .' He glanced at his watch. 'Where's the time gone? I was fetching the whisky . . .' He trailed off, and the hungry gaze was back on hers.

'Shall I bring it for you?'

Noting the huskiness in her own voice, Annabel drew away a little and turned her head towards the whisky bottle on the table. His hands at once closed on her wrists, holding her where she was, and when she turned back to him she was aware of nothing but the irresistible warmth of his touch through the silk of her shirt.

'I don't want any now.'

Holding her with his eyes, Caird flicked open the buttons at her wrists and raised her hands to his lips. Feeling his mouth on the sensitive inner flesh of each wrist in turn, she drew a long, trembling breath and let her fingers enjoy the hard squareness of his jaw, prickly now with a day's stubble. Then he was undoing the rest of her buttons, and the shirt was open wide, rustling away from her when she helped him to slide it from her shoulders. She leant towards him and the leather-clad arms encircled her, the zip of his jacket teasing her flesh while he undid the fastening of her bra. The lacy scrap loosened and dropped from breasts that had never needed its support. She looked down at them and, for the first time since suckling Sian, was proud of them, glad they had kept their shape and were so evenly tanned, glad too that she had never offered them like this to any man but Caird.

He pushed her gently back so that he could take their weight in his hands. Their crowns already stood high and assertive; she shuddered as he slowly moved his hands, stroking his fingers over the lower slopes and at last pressing the rosy peaks. Deep within her, a hot spring was opening, but for now her whole being was in these twin hills, jutting ever more dramatically as he worked them gently between fingers and thumbs.

'I could go on.' he said softly.

'I know.'

She didn't have to say more. She knew he was thinking as she was, of Sian left alone in a strange room.

'Just this, then.' He leant forward and raised her right breast to his lips for the softest of kisses.

'Theother one, too,' she begged.

So he left her right nipple, pink with fullness,

and turned to the other. She gasped, for he was curling his tongue round it, hardening his lips, showing the force of his desire, and the heat of that gushing spring was everywhere in her, carrying her in its headlong rush to an old, half-forgotten awareness of how much he meant to her.

Her fingertips ached with long-buried memories. Ached to take off his jacket and shirt, to feel again the contours of his shoulders, the springy softness of the hair on his chest. Her fingers yearned for the feel of him, had been yearning for so long that she had got used to it, accepted it as part of her life. But it wasn't, it needn't be, she only had to open this button, slide her hand in here and it was hers again, a great, rough, hot landscape for her to explore at leisure.

'Oh, my darling,' his voice came out muffled, his lips moving against her breast, 'I thought I remembered, but I didn't. Couldn't . . .'

What Annabel did next was the hardest thing she had ever done in her hard life. It needed all her strength, but she managed it, taking her hands from his body, drawing her breast from his mouth, rising shakily to her feet and standing, cold and alone again, a single creature that was made to be half of a pair. He slumped back and watched, heavy-eyed, as she shrugged herself quickly into her clothes.

'You're right, of course.' He took her hand, busy tucking her shirt into her jeans, and kissed the palm. 'Tomorrow, then?'

'All you want, my love,' she promised him, comforted by the contact and the reminder that there was always tomorrow. 'All we both want.'

CHAPTER SEVEN

BY SIX-THIRTY the following evening they were driving round the ancient walls of Frohnstadt. They had supper at an outdoor table on the dry, grassy bed of what had once been the moat, but Annabel wasn't at all hungry. She should have been; they had finished their lavish German breakfast at eight that morning and only paused for bread and cheese at lunch time, but she'd been in the driving seat too long. She felt as if she'd been driving all her life. Even crossing into Austria at Passau she'd been numb, unable to enjoy the luscious waterscape of the Danube with its two tributaries and wooded hills, though Caird made her stop specially to admire it.

She knew now she'd taken on far too much, travelling such a distance as sole driver with a child to look after. Thank goodness for Caird, who amused Sian and teased her and kept her occupied by showing her their progress across the map. He'd raced her at rest-stops, too, and made up games to while away the weary afternoon. How would they have managed without him?

The day had been close and overcast, with crackles of thunder on every horizon. Her long-sleeved shirt clung stickily to her as she shifted in her slatted metal chair, but the poached trout was superb, as were the buttered potatoes sprinkled with some fresh herb she didn't recognise.

'I'll ask what it is, if you like,' Caird said. 'But it probably doesn't grow in England.'

'Don't bother,' she told him, too tired even to be interested in cookery.

They refused wine. While Sian ate her ice-cream, Caird ordered two coffees, and Annabel was glad to sip the aromatic brew. It was ferociously strong, but that was all to the good. Twenty miles to go.

They started the last stage of their journey into an evening grown suddenly dark. The storm was over them at last, not raining yet, but with thunderheads piled up and ready for action. Annabel switched on the headlights, and saw the sign to Mauerdorf pointing up a narrow road which wound steeply through trees which shut off the last of the daylight. She changed gear doggedly, nerves alert to the sudden, complete silence in the back seat. Sian, who was so coolly unflustered by heights, strange animals, deep water, who could tackle the most complicated gymnastic feat with absolute courage, was terrified of thunderstorms.

Perhaps it would hold off till they reached Pankl's. She guided the car through the exacting curves of the climb and kept her mind on the road, but through her concentration was aware that Caird, too, had fallen silent. He was twisting in his seat now to look back at Sian, though he couldn't have seen much more than her outline by the pale glimmer of the instrument panel.

When he spoke, his voice held a soft, reassuring note. 'We often have deer crossing this road, half-pint.'

'D-deer?' with a barely conceal quaver. 'At n-night?'

'Specially at night—not that it's so late yet.'

It was in fact eight o'clock, time for the natural nightfall of these parts, even without the clouds and the overhanging trees. Annabel negotiated a bend in a white flicker of lightning, knowing what Caird was trying to do and grateful for it, but with little hope it would work. Sian always did her best to conceal her fear, but it was irrationally deep and strong. Over the years, Annabel had learnt Sian was seldom able to be distracted from it, though she could be comforted by human closeness. Being held tight and babied was what she needed at these times.

The road straightened a little and Annabel heaved an unconscious sigh, glad to be able to increase her speed a little. While the needle crept up to forty, she moved her shoulders, suddenly aware of the way she had been hunched over the wheel. But she was relaxing too soon; two patches of paler darkness broke from the general blackness of the trees, and her lights reflected green from two pairs of wide animal eyes. She jammed on the brakes, jerking both passengers forwards against their safety-belts, and stopped just short of a dappled doe and fawn, petrified in the glare of the headlights.

'Mummy, they're *frightened!*' Sian voice rose too high and thin on the last word. 'Stop them being so frightened, Mummy.'

In answer to Annabel's unspoken question,

Caird leant over to press the lights button. The merciless glare winked out, leaving a wall of darkness which gradually resolved itself into ordinary windy night, with the first rain plopping on the coachwork. The deer, mere patches of paleness again, stayed frozen for a second or two longer in front of the bonnet, then moved away into the woods on the other side of the road. The incident was over.

But the storm was only beginning. The lights when Annabel switched them on again were swamped for a second in a blinding flash, and the thunder followed so fast and loud it was obviously right overhead.

Annabel hesitated a moment before re-starting the engine. In the back, Sian was breathing hard, sniffing a little in the way that showed she was determinedly holding back tears. Caird heard it, too, exchanged another glance with Annabel in the dim glow of the instrument panel, and without speaking opened the door. A brief gust of rain blew round them as he straightened out of the front seat, tipped it forwards, and scrambled into the back. Annabel leant across to close the door and re-started the engine, knowing their daughter was being gathered in by those muscular arms, held against that solid chest, getting all the help she needed and never having to be shamed by her need for it because not a word had been spoken.

It was sensitively done, and just what they were both coming to expect of Caird. Annabel admitted it, pushing the car through the rattling, flashing darkness with hardly a care in the world because he was here to look after them. Perhaps he always could be. Perhaps they could be together for good . . . but no, she mustn't think about that now. It was too complicated and she had to get them through this forest, down this hill, across this wide valley the lightning had just picked out for her. The rain was really upon them now, battering their little glass and metal shell and bouncing from the road in splashes that streaked and shone in the headlights. Other, warmer lights glowed in the distance, but before she could see them more clearly Caird was giving her directions.

'Slow down. Now, turn right.'

She obeyed, and crawled up a rutted track to a white wall with wrought-iron gates set into it.

'Hang on.' Caird leant forward to climb out of the car. 'I'll open up.'

The yellow of the headlights and the white of the lightning showed the wind whipping his hair round his face. Not for long; it was soon plastered to his head by the rain as he fitted a key in the gate and turned it. Wet as a seal and smiling hugely, he set the gates back, flung an arm wide, and stepped aside so that she could edge past him in the direction he was indicating.

She came to a halt with the bonnet against a rough wall painted white. The lightning was obscured now and the thunder muffled by the roof she had driven under. Rain drummed overhead as she got out of the car and found they were in a long barn, walled on three sides and on the other open to a courtyard. A new flare of lightning showed more white wall, windowed this time, at the other side of the courtyard. Double steps with wrought-iron balustrades led up to a wide, dark door where Caird, his back turned, was presumably busy with another key.

Annabel leant into the car to push her seat forwards and stretch a hand into the darkness behind it. It was seized convulsively, as she had known it would be, by two small ones.

'Out you come, poppet,' she said softly, and was presently running through the rain with her daughter by the hand.

Up the steps, through the wide doorway, and they were under another roof. That was all she could tell in the complete, inky, most impenetrable darkness yet. Behind them, through the open doorway, the lightning still flashed, but showed nothing of their new surroundings except for one small window, briefly outlined in the same wall as the door and then surrendered once more to the general blackness.

A tiny, scraping sharpness penetrated the pattering hiss of the rain, and a match flared. Caird was lighting a candle, and when Annabel had closed the door to prevent the flame being blown out she saw that it was a fat red one on a dark saucer-shaped holder. Square emptiness was all its light showed, white walls, tiled floor, entries leading in every direction, and a tall cupboard with its flower-painted door half open.

'Here you are, half-pint, that's your candle.'

'Ooh!' Sian went forward to take it. 'Just like Christmas.'

Annabel opened her mouth to demand the

electric light, then closed it again as she realised there couldn't be any. The simple life without electricity was more than she'd bargained for, but she wasn't going to add to their troubles by saying so at this of all times. Instead, she accepted her own candle, yellow and globe-shaped, and watched Caird take a double bracket from the cupboard and light two more for himself.

'No, it isn't unfair,' he overruled Sian's protest, 'they're both thinner than yours. Besides, I have to light the stove.'

'Stove?' Annabel queried. 'In August?'

'To dry the building,' he explained briefly. 'Come on.'

He led them through the right-hand door into more huge emptiness, a bigger space than Annabel had ever seen before in any ordinary private house. It wasn't square this time, but shadowed with angles and corners. An enormous earthenware stove dominated one side, an open staircase went up another; cushioned benches filled one corner, round a table big enough to banquet ten, and a low divan at least five foot by seven stuck out invitingly from the slope under the stairs. The stove must have been ready laid, and skilfully, for Caird had it lit and crackling while Annabel and Sian were still exclaiming.

'These benches,' Annabel said. 'You could sleep two people just here, round the table.'

'They did, more or less.' He stood up and dusted off his hands. 'We added bedrooms in the roof-space, but until then this room was for sleeping, cooking, washing—it all happened here when the Pankls owned it.'

'Pankls!' Sian went off into a splutter of giggles. 'You mean, they were really called that?'

'Of course, tuppence, what did you think?'

'I thought . . .' Sian left her candle on the table to fling herself on the bench. 'I thought . . . it was just . . . your silly name,' she managed to explain between hiccups of laughter. 'Like calling me half-pint or tuppence . . . oh, dear!' She sat up, wiped her eyes on the back of her hand, and asked again to make quite sure, 'There really were people called Pankls?'

'Pankl.' He sat by her and put an arm round her, much as he must have done in the car when the thunder was bothering her, and spoke in much the same soothing murmur. 'I dare say they'd think Sian Stroud was just as funny.'

'I think somebody needs her sleep,' Annabel said.

'But *Mummy* . . .'

'All right, all right.' Annabel heard the panic thinly concealed in the routine protest, and hastened to reassure, 'We'll take our candles and explore first. Then Daddy . . .' hearing the word, she wondered why she had ever forbidden it ' . . . can show us how the cooker works, and we'll get you a hot drink . . .'

Behind Sian, Caird met Annabel's eyes and shook his head. She blinked, realising he didn't want to heat food and drink just now. Presumably his kitchen had some kind of solid fuel contraption like the stove he'd just lit, and would take hours to warm up to anything resembling cooking temperature. She glared back at him for not warning her about the inconveniences of this place, and went on pacifying Sian.

'And for tonight,' she carefully avoided referring to the storm, 'we'll put you down here, under the stairs. Then we'll be right here with you till you go to sleep.'

'Good idea.' Caird was opening two miniature iron doors in the stove. A scent of pine logs came out of it, and the room suddenly brightened with the dance of firelight. 'Have a look at the upstairs, half-pint,' he went on, 'and you can choose which room you want for later.'

Sian had picked up her candle before he finished speaking. She balanced it carefully towards the staircase, her trainers meeting the floorboards with quick, muted thumps, which reminded Annabel that the thunder hadn't sounded for quite a minute or two. While Caird went to fetch their overnight bags, she took her own candle and accompanied Sian up the stairs.

Their tiny lights showed a long landing, walled with built-in cupboards. Annabel slid one open and found slatted shelves full of bed linen, towels, tablecloths, a neatly folded pile of shirts. Good, so Caird had some dry clothes to change into.

The roof-space rooms were all unfurnished, save for beds. The three double rooms had slanting aluminium-framed windows let into the slope of the roof, the single had a casement where, intermittently lit by diminishing flashes of lightning, blue flowers tossed against the glass in their overgrown windowbox. Sian chose this room and would certainly make it her business later to tidy the windowbox. She set her candle on the windowsill and sat on the uncovered mattress, much braver now the storm was retreating.

'I expect, after I've finished with the bed downstairs,' she reminded her mother of where she was allowed to sleep tonight, 'you'll be wanting it.'

'Will I?' Annabel put her candle on the floor and joined her on the side of the bed. 'With all these rooms up here?'

'They won't do, will they?' Sian wasn't really asking, just confirming what she already knew to be true. 'The beds are like ours last night—singles put together.'

Annabel put an arm round her, glad to hear the chirpy little voice so cool and comfortable again. 'I expect I'll manage . . .'

'But if you're going to sleep with Father, you'll need the big one.'

'Oh.' Annabel heard her own voice hollow under the diminishing patter of the rain. 'But we're not married, darling.'

'Come on, Mummy, you weren't married when you made me.'

'That was a long time ago,' Annabel floundered, glad of the deep shadows to hide her blushes. It was one thing to tell the child, as accurately as possible within her understanding, how she came to be born; quite another to hear her bringing the whole process up to date. 'Shall we . . .'

'And you must have another baby, before

you're too old.'

'Sian . . .'

'Hayley shows off like anything about theirs.'

'You don't have babies so little girls can show them off.'

'You'd like it too, you know you would. You liked me when I was a baby.'

'But . . .'

'I haven't bothered you about it till now, have I?' Sian virtuously pointed out. 'But here we are with Father—you don't want to waste the chance.'

Not for the first time, Annabel saw the drawbacks of the way she had brought Sian up. It was all very well teaching her to work things out, answering all her questions honestly and helping develop her powers of independent reasoning. Only, every now and then, it led to something like this, a crazy tangle of misunderstanding that looked to a nine-year-old like simple common sense. It would take hours of explaining and arguing now to straighten her out—she always knew she was right, with all the confidence of one who had put the facts together for herself and drawn her own conclusions.

If I don't watch out, Annabel thought, she's going to turn into a right little know-all . . . she winced at the way that phrase kept coming back at her lately.

'It's . . . a big thing, having a baby,' she began slowly, but got no further.

'I know it isn't nice,' Sian was giving her hand a comforting pat. 'We've watched Midnight and Sable heaps of times.'

Annabel was once more robbed of speech. She had always wanted Sian to know the facts of life as naturally and straightforwardly as possible, so in the past had listened patiently to stories from the livery stables. What she hadn't bargained for was the uncluttered nine-year-old view of the proceedings, now becoming ever clearer as Sian went on.

'It must be worse than being injected. Sable carries on like anything . . . '

'Human beings aren't horses,' Annabel interrupted in desperation, and, because that didn't seem the right approach either, she added, 'You'll . . . you'll understand it better when you're grown up.'

'And it must hurt even worse when the baby comes out.'

Annabel nodded, remembering. 'But it's absolutely marvellous, too.'

'You see? So it's well worth the trouble of being with Father in the double bed.'

'That's enough, Sian.' Annabel was thankfully aware of feet ascending the stairs and the glow of candles along the corridor. 'Here he is. Let's all go down and . . . '

'Father, I'm just explaining to Mummy about the beds.'

'Oh, yes?' Caird looked enormous in the shifting shadows as he put his candlestick on the windowsill beside Sian's

'Come on,' Annabel accepted the overnight bag and unzipped it, 'you can put your pyjamas on now.'

'Have I got to wash?' Sian asked.

Annabel wondered briefly how that was done here—in the kitchen, no doubt, with buckets. She looked at Caird. 'Do you have to go outside for your water?'

His mouth twitched in the wavering gold of the candles. 'The bathroom's right next to you, here.'

Annabel was silent, digesting the information and readjusting her ideas. It was Sian who spoke next, glad of the chance to pursue her objective of the moment.

'You and Mummy'll need the double bed downstairs, to make the new baby.'

His amused glance met Annabel's. 'And what does your mother say about that?'

'Don't blame me,' she answered, less flustered already by his light, matter-of-fact tone. 'She worked this out all by herself.'

'Right.' He was suddenly practical. 'You'd better mind your own business, half-pint.'

'But it *is* my business. A new baby . . .'

'Would be very nice for you, and a lot of work and worry for your mother.'

'I'd help . . .'

'When you felt like it. When you weren't riding, or mucking out the stables, or staying late for gym practice.'

'I could make the time,' she persisted indignantly. 'A new baby's not just anything . . .'

'It is not. You're out of your depth, half-pint.' The steel was back in Caird's voice, closing the discussion like a door clanging shut. 'What about having a look at my bathroom? It's the latest thing we've done to the place.'

It turned out to be enormous, tiled in spring green, a figured tile here and there patterned with pine trees. A round pine-green bath filled one corner.

'Not what I'd have chosen,' he assured them as Sian rushed to try the gold dolphin taps. 'But I thought, let Becky . . .' He checked himself abruptly, looked away, continued on a new breath, 'I thought, let's have a bit of luxury, just for once.'

The sour taste surged back into Annabel's throat as she noted for the first time the bottle of Heather cologne above the wash-basin. He'd talked of the bathroom as 'the latest thing we've done.' She understood that 'we' now—this Becky had clearly chosen the fittings here, and was presumably still about.

Well, had she expected him to be living like a monk? She realised with dismay that this was exactly what she had expected—hadn't he assured her several times, with that damned air of honesty he could put on so easily, that he didn't sleep around? She had taken him to mean no women in his life, which only showed how she would never learn any sense where he was concerned. She had quite forgotten how easily he would form loving relationships with women.

And he had one now, with a woman called Becky. His eyes had been full of affection, adoration almost, as he'd spoken the name, and after it he'd halted too abruptly, trying to pretend he'd never mentioned it all. What was he hiding?

Annabel stared at the cologne until it blurred

and fatigue suddenly swept over her. What could he be hiding but a bond already forged, and one he didn't want her to know about? What did he intend to do—drop Becky and send her packing with her cologne? Or take the chance of Becky being out of the way, and amuse himself for a fortnight with his suddenly acquired family?

It was so like what had happened ten years ago. He said he was already divorced before they met, but how could she believe him now? That marvellous moment last night when they'd seemed so close, so much of the same mind as they longed for the unity of their bodies and held back because of their love for their daughter—how much of that had been real, and how much had she simply been fooling herself? And, even if it had all been real, that was wrong too, because in committing himself to her like that he was conveniently forgetting another woman called Becky.

'Towels,' he was back from the landing cupboard, 'and soap.' He brought his candlestick near the wash-basin and disclosed a dark green tablet which until then had been invisible against its dark green background.

Sian picked it up and sniffed. 'It smells a bit like your fire downstairs.'

'Pinus silvestris,' he confirmed, 'to match the forest, I believe was the idea.'

He had spoken with a note of mockery, but it was a tender mockery. Whoever this Becky was, he . . . loved her. Annabel swallowed down more sourness.

'It's a bit lush for you, all this.' She wasn't going

to ask about the woman who'd planned it, but she couldn't help giving him the opening. He could tell her more if he chose.

He didn't. 'There won't be any hot water yet. Can Sian have a lick and a promise, just for tonight?'

Annabel nodded wearily. 'I'll get her toothbrush.'

Really, she thought grouchily as she trailed back to the bathroom with their toilet bag, what kind of priorities had he? A luxury bathroom, when he had no electricity and his only heating was a wood-burning stove. His kitchen was probably a horror of a primus or Calor gas or solid fuel; he wouldn't have a fridge or any other of the comforts you normally took for granted. Why, he didn't even seem to have proper oil lamps, just these stupid ornamental candles, and not enough of those.

She supervised Sian's change into her night attire in a general haze of exhaustion. When they came downstairs again, candles aloft, they found a huge duvet cover spread on the divan beneath the stairs, and Caird fitting a double duvet into it.

'Does she need one that big?' Annabel enquired, and was met with a long, oblique glance from the shadowed eyes.

'It's the one we always put on this bed.'

He uses it with Becky, I suppose, she thought, hating its luxurious softness and faint scent of pinus silvestris that rose from it. She grasped it firmly and pulled it back. 'Right madam, in you go.'

Sian climbed in without protest. It wasn't like going to bed at all really, when she could stay down here where everything was going on. She didn't even ask for her book, which was just as well, because she couldn't have read it by candlelight. Taking both candles from the open stair where she had put them, Annabel noticed for the first time a shaded bracket on the wall above the pillows. An oil lamp, perhaps? It didn't seem too safe a place, perhaps that was why Caird hadn't offered to light it.

But wait a minute, wasn't that a switch next to it? It was, a square modern electric switch. From her seat on the bed she looked into the room and saw other switches, yes, and more wall brackets above the table and either side of the fire. A four-armed wooden chandelier hung from the ceiling, its glass bulbs shaded but still visible in the firelight.

A distant flicker of lighting, the tail of the storm, outlined the windows for a moment and gave her the answer. A power cut. Perhaps the storm had brought some cables down, or perhaps the place had a generator which needed connecting up somehow, and Caird had left that until he'd got Sian settled and happy. Which she certainly was, blinking owlishly from her pillow and almost asleep already.

Annabel bent down to nuzzle the soft cheek, scented with pinus silvestris. Sian sighed, breathed in deeply, and as usual turned on her side, facing the wall. She was away for the night, leaving Annabel alone with Caird and all the question she might, or might not, ask him.

CHAPTER EIGHT

'WHAT did you expect me to say?' Caird asked. 'That we'd a power failure and I didn't know why, it just happens sometimes?'

They were in the kitchen, where he was opening a bottle of Austrian beer. The light of their candles flickered on dish-washer, freezer, fridge, electric stove, and endless gleaming work-surfaces. The rain still rattled sporadically and the wind still tossed the flowers in the window boxes, but much less. It looked as if the storm would blow itself out before midnight.

Annabel warmed her brandy balloon and breathed in the vapour from the spoonful of brandy she had put in it. She had to admit he'd been right to avoid fussing about the power failure; in fact, he had coped with it very well. She knew now he had tried a switch on first entering the hall, and when the light didn't respond had gone at once to the cupboard. By the time she and Sian were with him he had located candles and matches from memory, and was ready to use them as if they were the only lights he expected.

Annabel knew, too, that her opening remarks just now about the electricity had been aggressive. She couldn't help it, she felt such a fool when she could see everywhere that the house had a perfectly normal power supply. Switches, sockets, a striplight in the bathroom—how could she have overlooked them all? And, as Caird was pointing out, he couldn't have told them about the power failure without worrying Sian still further.

'I'm sorry,' she apologised reluctantly. 'I didn't mean you *ought* to have told me. It's just . . .'

'You're tired, love.'

She turned away impatiently, refusing to answer. He called all women 'love', it was just a word. Perhaps the others didn't mind too much, but she didn't want to hear it unless he meant it.

'It's a long way to drive,' he went on. 'Too far maybe, in your little car.'

This had been exactly her own conclusion, but she only bristled further. Who did he think he was patronising? 'Yes, well, it might have been easier if we hadn't . . .'

Got mixed up with you, she'd meant to say, but couldn't. It wasn't true. Certainly he'd involved them in the ugly incident with Denny, but he'd made up for that several times over by his guidance on the route, his interpreting at their stops, above all by his help with Sian. Without him, it wouldn't have been easier, it would have been harder.

'. . . if we hadn't run into the storm,' she finished lamely.

What was the matter with her, why was she snapping at every harmless thing he said? She knew the answer to that, but it was a hard one to face. 'What are you going to do about it?' she asked to distract herself, and nodded towards the electric stove. 'We won't even be able to have coffee in the morning . . .'

'Yes, we will, I've found the camping gaz burner.'

'You get a lot of power failures, then?'

'Now and again—I think there's a faulty connection.' He took a tray from the wall and put their glasses on it, along with his candles. 'Shall we go and relax for a minute?'

Sian's candle burnt peacefully where they had left it on the big table. She was almost invisible in the shadows, but as they entered with their extra lights she moved and murmured in her sleep. Caird led the way to the table and left his tray there while he refuelled the stove. Its red glow darkened for a moment with the fresh logs, but they must have been very dry; they caught almost at once in a crackle of sparks and added their wavering gold to the steadier glow of the candles.

Annabel dropped thankfully to the cushioned bench. When she picked up her glass and sniffed it again, the heady fumes seemed to rise right into her brain and cloud it worse than ever. She closed her eyes, nodding over the table, until a soft movement near her raised the hair at the nape of her neck. She dragged her eyes open with difficulty and found them resting on narrow, denimed hips. Caird was standing by her, she discovered, and let her eyes wander above his leather belt to the checked cotton shirt which covered his broad chest and shoulders. She wondered muzzily when he'd changed into dry clothes. He must have towelled his hair at the

same time, it was springing up in clumps, even
more rebellious than usual after its recent wetting.

'Make room.' he murmured, so gently that it
didn't seem like an order.

She obeyed with a sleepy heaviness, and reset-
tled at the further corner of the table. When he
lowered himself next to her, she couldn't help
noticing the inches of empty space he chose to
leave between them. Perhaps he was remembering Becky, and having second thoughts. It was just
as well, anyway, she wouldn't make any sense at
all if he touched her, and she needed to make
sense. There were so many questions to be
answered.

'Listen, love,' that damned endearment again,
yet sounding so natural and right, 'you're worn
out. Why don't you drink that down and . . .'

'The electricity . . ' she trailed off, her mind fixed
to its treadmill like a weary donkey.

'What can we do about that tonight, silly?'

'It's a worry, though . . .'

'No, it isn't. I'll get Otto here in the morning.'

'Otto?'

'A man in the village. He keeps an eye on the
place when we aren't here . . .'

'*We?*'

Her eyes snapped and she jerked round in time
to see him catching his lower lip in his teeth, his
hand slapping the table in annoyance at himself.
Yet when he turned to her in the candlelight his
face showed no guilt, nothing but an interest in
and concern for herself.

'It isn't really we. When *I'm* not here, I should

have said.'

He didn't look as if he was lying. Annabel remembered how very closely Sian took after him, and how truthful her daughter had always been. Besides, Annabel reckoned that in four years of free-lance catering, she had learnt to spot somebody who couldn't be trusted—with no other income, she'd had to. And everything about Caird, her whole experience of him on this trip, said he was utterly dependable. But then, that was exactly what she'd felt about him ten years ago.

Why did he so much regret having used the word we? It had to be Becky he was thinking of. And why did he not want to talk about Becky? If he wouldn't tell her, she wouldn't ask—yet her throat ached with not asking.

'We've so much to sort out, love.' He was pouring the rest of his beer, watching the bubbles shoot up to a head of foam gilded by the candlelight. 'And I never seem to get you to myself.'

'The last time we were alone,' she said slowly, 'we didn't talk at all.'

'I know.' He gave her a sidelong glance. 'You must have noticed, I'm trying not to get carried away like that now.'

'W-why not?' Try as she might, she couldn't keep the wistfulness out of her voice. If he would come closer, put an arm round her, let her rest her head on his shoulder, everything might be easier. And, if the closeness led to his making love, it would at least be something. A memory to treasure in the long future without him.

He was staring at her with a hint of exasperation. 'You honestly don't know why not? When Sian reminded us an hour ago?

'Oh. You mean, a baby?'

'We've done it once, haven't we?' The deep-set eyes tore themselves away from hers. 'You're a grown woman now. You know what it all means.'

'Yes.' She took a sip of her brandy, tasting only bitterness. 'Very sensible.'

Deep inside her, the pain nagged on. He loved the daughter she had already borne him, but he didn't want another child. Didn't want the responsibility, wasn't ready to make the commitment. Had another woman in his life, called Becky.

She spoke convulsively, out of a need to stifle the pain. 'How do you know I'm not . . . protected?'

'Are you?'

He turned quickly towards her, and she couldn't mistake the hope, the hunger in that gesture. Yet something else in it was harder to explain—could it be disappointment? Would he be disappointed to learn that she kept herself prepared for possible romantic encounters? And if so, why?

She shook her head in slow denial. No, she wasn't prepared. She could have lied to him the way she'd done ten years ago, but, as he'd just pointed out, she was a grown woman now. She knew the crushing responsibilities a baby brought; in her present life, it would turn all her plans upside-down, and she and Sian would both suffer. She couldn't risk it.

'Oh, my love,' he had taken her hand and was kissing each finger in turn, 'somehow I knew you wouldn't be.'

'How?' Two desires fought in her. She wanted to leave her hand in his, bring the other one over to run it through that tufty-dried hair, let it explore the shape of his head, the ears, the strong neck. But she fought that because she wanted also to hurt him. Why should he have his Becky and expect her to have nobody? She snatched her hand away. 'How do you know I haven't a regular lover, back home?'

He pulled a rueful face. 'Let's just say, I hoped . . . have you finished that brandy yet?'

'No.' She held it and sniffed it, determined to go to bed in her own good time.

'I thought you might bunk down here with Sian for tonight,' he went on easily. 'Then we'll sort ourselves out tomorrow.'

'I want to sort ourselves out now.' She stared into her glass. Damn him, was he never going to tell her about his Becky?

'If you must.' He drained his beer, put down the glass, and turned to face her with a serious expression. 'Here's what I have in mind. You live in Rybridge, right?'

She nodded, mystified.

'And it suits you there?'

'It's all right,' she admitted reluctantly, perplexed by what seemed his abrupt change of direction. 'A nice little town. I suppose I'm happy enough there . . . now.'

'You mean, you weren't at first?'

'I had a hard time,' she reminded him sharply. 'But . . . Sian likes her school. The air's clean, the country's near . . .'

'Sounds like heaven.'

'Well, it isn't' she said ungraciously, 'but it's all right.'

'You'd recommend it, then?'

'Who to?' Completely lost now, she stared at him, and found him unreadable in the shadows.

'I'm not making much of a job of this,' he said at last. 'That's why I didn't want to start it tonight.'

'What are you trying to say?'

He sighed and pushed his glass away. 'I've finished my contract. I'm not renewing.'

'You mean,' she tried to take it in, 'no more radio? Or television, either?'

'The television was only a spin-off—I didn't really like it.' He kept his eyes on his empty glass, his profile set and sad. 'I'm getting too old, love.'

'At thirty-seven?'

'All right, then, let's just say I've broken too many bones. It's somebody else's turn.'

'And . . .' She paused, bewildered to find how inseparably linked they were in her mind, Caird and his programme. 'And they've got a new presenter?'

He shook his head. 'They're taking it off.'

'It can't be losing audiences . . .'

'It isn't. It's losing me.'

She was silent, trying to sort out the implications of what he'd told her. So, just as she had always believed, he was the programme and the programme was him; without him, it would stop. But when it stopped, where did that leave him, thirty-seven and unemployed?

'I'll be all right.' He grinned, reading some of the questions she was trying to frame. 'You must have noticed, I'm not short of a bob or two.'

'Enough to live on for the rest of your life?' she queried, unable to believe in that much money in one bank account.

'More than, the way I live.'

She could see that. He had no taste for luxury, never had. He dressed simply, ran a car that was good but nowhere near the millionaire bracket, and preferred places with character to places with what she thought of as gloss. That was why he had bought this solid, comfortable farmhouse, which was probably gaining in value all the time, when he might have been flying to hotels in the Bahamas or living it up in any of the world's great cities. And it wasn't because he cared about money or wanted to save it. He just couldn't be bothered with the more complicated ways of spending it.

'Only, just living isn't enough, is it? she asked carefully. 'You'll have to do something.'

'I've been thinking about that.' He frowned, working on it. 'It'll have to be quite different. Something to do with land, I think. Did you know my old dad runs a market garden?'

'Couldn't you take it over, then? Or help?'

He shook his head, his smile full of affection. 'I had in mind something bigger than that—a country park, perhaps. Besides, Dad's only fifty-eight.'

'He must have been very young when you were born.'

'He nodded. 'We breed early, us Glosters.'

'I'm not surprised,' she snapped.

'Right.' He stood up and stretched, his shadow flickering, complex and gigantic, across the floor. 'I'm off to bed, then.'

'But . . . but . . .' Annabel floundered, wanting to keep him with her, wanting to know more, yet unable to get her stubborn tongue round an honest request for a little more time with him. 'But I'm not sleepy yet . . .'

'You never are.' He laughed softly. 'Do you think I've forgotten? You're just like her,' he gestured to the slumbering figure in the corner, 'put it off till the last minute, and drop off while you're still fighting it.'

'But I'll never sleep, with all this . . .'

'You won't talk about it, either.' He had let his arms fall to his sides, but he wasn't making any move to sit down again. 'You've gone back to the way you were before. Scoring points instead of really talking.'

He went to put more wood on the stove, filling it right up and closing its doors. In the deeper gloom that came with the shutting off of the flames, she drained the last trickle of her brandy and faced the truth of what he'd just told her. She had indeed gone back to fencing with him, meeting his most harmless comments with aggressive back-answers which got them nowhere. And, yes, he was right, she'd done a lot of that when she first ran into him. She couldn't say exactly when she'd stopped, only that somewhere in the course of this journey she had relaxed and begun to trust him.

And now she didn't any more. How could she, when she'd given him endless openings to tell her about his Becky, and he hadn't taken any of them? You could always ask him, the voice at the back of her mind told her, and she resisted it stubbornly. He was going to tell her by his own choice, or not at all.

And what was this talk about Rybridge? Did he intend to come and live there? And if he did, what could it mean but . . . no, she mustn't let herself think about that. It was too good to be true. She could easily imagine him drawn to the small-town cosiness of Rybridge after the rackety life he'd clearly grown tired of. And if he was thinking of moving, he'd be bound to consider a place close enough for him to keep in touch with Sian. Knowing Sian was what mattered to him, had been ever since he discovered her existence. He'd never made any secret of it. The other thing, the attraction between Caird and herself—well, he'd referred to it as 'unfinished business', and that probably just about summed up his feelings for her. They'd been together for two days now, never alone, never with a chance to give in to their desires. So of course he wanted her, she didn't doubt that. Just as he'd wanted her ten years ago, just as he'd probably wanted any number of women before and since.

Whereas she—Annabel faced it at last—she wanted him and only him. Always had. Her need for him had wrecked her life once, and now was coming pretty close to wrecking it again, if she let it. And only one thing could stop it; she had to get herself and Sian on their way in the morning. She had kept her word, brought him to his farmhouse. Let him enjoy it now, with or without his Becky; he couldn't expect Annabel to hang around and allow the whole painfully achieved balance of her life to be destroyed again as it had been ten years ago.

Yes, she would go in the morning, move on, after all, to Salzburg.

Something was happening. The table was moving away from under her arms, just when she'd got them nicely folded, to rest her head on them. It was a shame if you couldn't rest your head on your arms and think a little, without somebody pulling the table from under you . . .

'What are you doing?'

She meant it to be forceful, to register her objection to being picked up like this, but it came out all wrong. He had one arm under her knees, the other round her waist, and it felt so good just to loll against him and not worry any more. So he was going to make love to her, after all. So be it, his choice, not her fault. She couldn't stop him when she was nearly asleep, could she? She snuggled into his shoulder and smiled. No doubt he'd wake her up when the time came.

So smooth, so smooth, the way his springy stride carried them both to wherever he was taking them. Sure enough, it was a bed. She was able to stetch full length on it, and pull the pillow under her cheek, while a light soft cover dropped over her, and it was dark . . .

And it was morning. Sunlight flooded the corner where the table stood, still littered with bottles and glasses and half-burnt candles, and still askew as he'd pulled it. Near it, by the bench where she'd been sitting, her own sandals lay exactly as she must have eased her feet out of them some time last night. They were the only item she'd managed to take off before she went to sleep; for the rest, she had spent the night in the same clothes she'd worn all day. She looked down with distaste at the dark long-sleeved shirt she'd put on fresh for the evening at the Sonne and then worn for a long day's journey. It was anything but fresh now.

She must change it. She must shower, even if the water was still cold, and so must Sian—but where was Sian? Only a crumpled pillow showed where she had been sleeping. She must have risen without disturbing her mother, and now be around the place getting up to goodness knew what. Annabel could hear noises from outside, the open window let in the sounds of voices, and of car doors opening and shutting.

A few minutes later Caird came in, draped about with the three soft travelling bags bought specially for Neddy. 'Welcome back,' he smiled across at her. 'Take all the time you want—we're sorting things out.'

He padded up the stairs, and Sian arrived with Annabel's document wallet and their two sets of waterproofs. She too was wearing yesterday's clothes; she must have scrambled back into them as she found them.

'I wanted to wake you,' she came over to the bed and bounced down on it, 'but Daddy said no.'

'What time is it?' Annabel struggled to sit up, and realised she was still wearing her wrist-watch, as well as everything else. It was just gone eight.

'We've been up for hours.' Sian was superior for a moment, until enthusiasm got the better of her. 'There's a forest up the hill. And wild raspberries, and blueberries, and mushrooms . . . '

'Very interesting.' Annabel stretched and yawned, realising how tired she still was. 'Have you washed?'

'Mummy, how can you go on about washing, when we're in this marvellous place . . .'

She went on to reveal more of its marvels. If Mummy would get up and look through the windows, she'd see all the way down to the village. The church had a green and gold sort of bulb-thing on top, which Daddy said was an onion dome. There was an inn, too, the Adler—wasn't that a funny word?—it meant eagle, so they were all going to have breakfast in the Eagle. Then they would see Otto about the electricity, buy butter and eggs and things, and then . . .

'Then,' her eyes shone, 'we're going to the livery stables.'

Annabel slumped back on her pillow. It would take more than one night's sleep to get her over the strain of this journey. As for moving on the way she'd been planning last night, she could scarcely believe she'd thought of it seriously. With Sian this attached to the place already, how could she ever be winkled out of it? Anything else they did was going to seem like a very poor subsitute— to both of them.

Yes, to both of them, she admitted with her eyes shut and Sian still prattling. Whatever the complications raised by this other woman, this Becky, whatever secret Caird was hiding from her, she still wanted to be with him. More, she felt honoured to be here in this home he'd made for himself. She liked it as much as Sian did, and wanted the chance to explore it. It was his own secret hiding-place, where he could get right away from the cares of his usual life, and she was glad to be sharing it with him.

With him and Becky? She threw the covers back; she'd better things to do than lie there worrying over that one.

She found their bags in Sian's chosen bedroom upstairs. Fishing out a clean pair of jeans and another long-sleeved shirt, she paused, left them, and delved instead for the sleeveless sea-blue top which showed off her tan. And what about the matching pleated skirt to make the outfit look like a dress—why not be a woman for once? By the time she had showered in the plentiful hot water, she was feeling almost optimistic. Blow-drying her hair in her usual way, by running her fingers through it, she inspected herself in the corridor mirror. She looked healthy and nicely turned out—maybe even just a little bit pretty.

'Wow!' Evidently Caird thought so, too, coming up from below to see if she was ready. 'You managed all that in ten minutes?'

She was about to retort that she'd packed this outfit for Salzburg, but she bit it off in time. No more fencing; he was saying something nice and she would respond in the same way.

She smiled and turned to him as he approached. 'I'm hungry. What was that about breakfast in the village?'

'I'm hungry, too.' He clearly didn't mean for food.

She looked at him in exasperation. 'You do pick your times, don't you?'

'They pick me.'

He ran a hand up the smooth, bronzed top of her arm, so that she shivered and started away from him. With Sian downstairs and all sorts of things to be attended to, she wasn't going to think at all about how he made her feel when he did things like that. It was complicated enough already, even before she had the great unanswered question of Becky hanging over her. But, in spite of her busy, resentful thoughts as she ran downstairs, her tingling arm felt more alive than all the rest of her body.

Once they had cut across the still-wet meadow to the road, the walk to Mauerdorf took ten minutes. The only traffic to pass them in that time was an old lady on a bicycle, who nodded in courteous greeting. It was that kind of place, Caird explained as they wandered along the wide village street, you just said hello to everyone you met.

The Alder stood opposite the church, flanked by enough shops to set Annabel's mind at rest about provisons to take back to the farm. They breakfasted on cold meat, mountains of crusty rolls, and more of that delicious Austrian coffee which, like last night's, was so strong you couldn't afford to drink much of it. While they were pouring it, a ruddy-cheeked man wandered in, slung his green felt hat on a peg, and was introduced as Otto. He shook hands with all of them, including the delighted Sian, and accepted a cup of coffee from their pot while he and Caird conferred in German. Then he shook hands all round again before ambling out.

'You'll get used to it,' Caird told Sian. 'They always shake hands here. Little girls like you learn to curtsy as well.'

Annabel cut into Sian's exclamations. 'Where's Otto gone?'

'Goodness knows,' Caird said easily. 'He'll be up at Pankl's presently, though. If he can't put it right, we'll call the Electricity Board.'

Annabel hoped Otto knew what he was doing, but didn't say so. As usual after food, she was feeling much more optimistic and at peace with the world. The electricity would be fixed, and if it wasn't they still had candles and camping gaz. As for the other thing, she was just being silly. The minute she got Caird to herself again—perhaps while Sian was riding, or after she'd gone to bed this evening—they must sort that out. If he didn't tell her, she'd swallow her stupid pride and ask him, straight out, who Becky was.

But, as it happened, she didn't need to do that. When they returned to the farm with their plastic sacks of groceries, the gates had been thrown open, and a battered blue Volkswagen Beetle was parked beside Neddy under the cover of the barn. Annabel took it for Otto's until she saw how Caird's eyes sought the house with eager delight, a pleasure so intense that his normal easy-going smile was lost in it. He'd forgotten her and Sian completely; his whole attention was at the top of the steps, where a beautiful redhead stood looking down at them.

CHAPTER NINE

'BECKY!' Caird leapt up the steps, his broad back hiding the girl as he drew her close. 'I hoped you might come . . .'

Annabel's first feeling was a huge numbness. She realised she was no longer surprised by his having another woman in his life—she had almost come to terms with that. But one he cared for so much he couldn't wait to get his arms round her, one who made him forget her and Sian completely—that was something she hadn't reckoned with.

And no wonder, she told herself, no wonder she hadn't been prepared for it. He'd been stringing her along during this whole trip. Right from the first moment they had met again, he'd shown he still wanted her, had seized every chance to make love. Worse, much worse, he'd almost convinced her she was important to him. Why, when he talked last night of a change in his life-style, she had thought . . .

Well, she could forget that, couldn't she? She'd clearly been mistaken, and it was herself she ought to be angry with. In this numb detachment that wouldn't let go of her, a favourite saying of her wayward mother's floated into her mind. 'If a man lets you down once, it's his fault. If he lets you down twice, it's your fault for giving him the chance.' And she knew a thing or two about men, my mother, Annabel thought with a distant bitterness. I could have learnt something from her.

But she hadn't learnt, not from her mother's life, not from her own, and now she must pay. This numbness was only temporary; already it was beginning to lift and free the pain, misery, rage that lay banked beneath it. When those really took hold of her she would learn properly and learn well, she'd have no choice.

But that wasn't happening quite yet. For now, she still had enough self-possession to take in the details of Becky's appearance as it emerged from Caird's embrace. Glinting red-gold hair blew about her shoulders, jeans and T-shirt set off her leggy slenderness, and her neat, lightly freckled features were enviably young, enviably poised and unruffled by this horribly awkward situation. None of Caird's excitement was reflected in her face, though she was warming a little to his welcome. Her glance met Annabel's and lingered with an interest curiously unconcerned, as if she took it for granted he would have an extra woman in tow. Almost, she might have been pleased by it. Maybe this was her secret, the special quality which kept her and Caird together. Maybe she was so sure of him, and so sure of herself, she just genuinely didn't mind other women. After all, he was so obviously hers whenever she wanted him.

The cool stare altered though, as it rested on Sian. And well it might—when the child stood like that, feet apart and hands in pockets, hazel eyes on the newcomer with open, friendly curiosity, there was no mistaking whose daughter she was. That, at least, was giving this sophisticated young woman something to think about.

Becky turned back to Caird. 'How about some introductions?'

Her light American voice was questioning, but still detached. And when you came to think of it, why should she worry? She needn't have the slightest doubt of her own hold on his affections, and Sian was nine years old—whatever passion brought her into the world, it had all been a long time ago.

I'm a has-been, Annabel thought bitterly, a mere piece of his past she'll be interested to hear about.

'Eh?' At least Caird was looking uncomfortable. 'Oh. Yes, I suppose I'd better. Annabel, this is . . .'

'Becky.' Sian cut in. 'You did Daddy's bathroom. He told us about you last night.'

'He did? The cool glance was back on Caird. 'Well, well! I can see I've a little catching up to do.'

'You certainly have,' he confirmed. 'That's Sian, and she's sometimes a bit big for her boots . . .'

'Have you gone and got married while my back was turned?'

Annabel blinked at the light, teasing note of the question. Becky must be very, very sure of Caird, to be able to make jokes like that. Perhaps the question was a little malicious, drawing attention to his embarrassment, but if so who could blame her?

Good for her, Annabel thought savagely, numbness gone and pain sweeping in to take its place,

I only wish it was me able to upset him like that!

'Er—look, love,' Caird was using that damned endearment again, and for Becky, 'I didn't mean it to happen like this, but it has, and I'd better tell you the rest.' He laid a possessive hand on her waist. 'Supposing we go to the kitchen? I expect you'd be glad of some coffee . . .' His voice faded as he steered her into the house.

And that was it. Off with the old, on with the new. Or rather, off with the temporary and back to the lasting, the tolerant, the understanding, the woman he preferred above all others, partly because she didn't mind about the others. He would be sitting her down in that gleaming kitchen, seeing to her needs in his practical, easy way, and explaining how it all happened. Sure of a sympathetic hearing, sure nothing would be blown up out of proportion, sure that his precious Becky would accept this as she accepted all his little ways, serenely and without fuss.

If she could do that, she was indeed a woman in a million. But it still hurt, that Becky was the one he was thinking about now, that it was to Becky he was making his explanations. Annabel felt cold iron beneath her palm and realised she was climbing the steps, pulling herself up by the wrought-iron hand-rest of the balustrade, trailing the butter and the eggs in their plastic sack as if they were too heavy for her to lift.

'Here,' she dumped them on the floor in the hall, 'take these to the kitchen, will you?'

Following her in, Sian nodded and picked them

up. 'I shall like having Becky here, won't you? She looks nice.'

'And when you've done that, come upstairs to the bathroom. I want you washed and changed before we . . .'

Annabel left her sentence unfinished. They had to move on, of course, they couldn't stay here any longer, but she hated to think of the trouble she was going to have with Sian. It might be cowardly, but she couldn't face all the arguments just yet. One thing at a time.

Luckily, the child hadn't noticed. 'Look,' she was pointing to the hall lantern, 'the light's on. We've got electricity!'

Annabel noted it with lack-lustre agreement, and switched it off. Otto must have been very quick to trace the fault and repair it.

'I'll just see if Daddy knows.'

Sian moved importantly to the kitchen, where the door was firmly closed—whatever was going on in there must be very private. Annabel opened her mouth to tell her leave it for now, then closed it again without speaking, and dragged herself across the hall towards the living-room with its stairs. Let them send Sian away if they didn't want her.

And send her away was exactly what they did. She appeared upstairs a minute or two later, cheerful enough.

'Daddy says we're to go back in ten minutes. Coffee then, he says, if you want it.'

'He can keep it,' Annabel snapped and bit her lip when she saw the child's puzzled face.

She mustn't take this out on Sian. Maybe presently she'd go down and accept that coffee after all, and pour it straight over Caird's head—that would be putting her anger where it did most good! Meanwhile, she had plenty to occupy her, repacking the overnight bag, checking downstairs for anything she might have left there, planning their route on the map, seeing Sian caught up with the shower she'd missed yesterday—all the small things that went to make up a busy, empty life without him.

She sent her daughter off to the bathroom and went through her tasks mechanically, trying not to think. What a good thing she hadn't unpacked too much, and so wasn't forced to go gathering their possessions from every corner of this cursed place. The main luggage was still in its bags, and only one of them needed tidying and compressing—the one she'd sorted through to take out this shirt and top she was wearing.

To think that only an hour ago she'd decided to dress like a woman for once. She'd felt like a woman, too, let him through her defences to plague her with longings she thought she'd mastered years ago. Yes, he'd managed to set her on fire again, just as if the years between had never existed, but that was the least of it.

Worse, far worse, was the deception. He'd made her think he cared for her and her only, and so had brought her to admit at last that she cared for him. He'd fooled her so completely, she'd started to look seriously at those glimpses he'd given her of a different life she might be leading.

And how could she resist them? After the years

of lonely struggle, how could she turn away from the thought of a partnership, where problems were shared? Where she could help, comfort, love the man of her choice, because he needed her. Where he was always there, strong and loving and reliable . . .

Reliable! Yes, here it was, she thought with rising fury, this was the real damage he'd done. He'd persuaded her to trust him. How could she have been such a fool, when her whole life had taught her never to trust anybody but herself? But he had broken it down completely, that self-reliance which had helped her this far. All the protective hardness, the owing-nothing-to-anybody pride which had taken her so many painful years to build, all had softened and dropped away from her in the last day or two, and she'd allowed herself to dream. Allowed herself to hope . . .

She jerked the sea-blue top over her head, dropped the pleated skirt round her feet, and pulled from the bag the jeans she'd rejected earlier. With them came a clean long-sleeved shirt, a sombre olive-green to match her mood. When they were girded round her, she flung the sea-blue outfit back into the bag as if she owed it a grudge, and closed the zip with a noise like something being ripped apart.

'Don't bother unpacking just now, Mummy.' Sian was back from the bathroom already, hair swathed in a towel. 'After we've been to the stables, I'll help.'

Annable unwrapped the towel and plied it

mechanically with all her usual thoroughness. Rubbing the worst of the wetness from the fine, short hair, feeling the small, precious head beneath her fingers, she gathered her courage.

'Right,' she said when the drying and dressing were completed. 'Now listen. We're going away from here.'

'What?' Sian jerked round, all attention. 'We're not!'

Annabel sighed, facing the trouble she had foreseen. 'I said I'd bring you here, and I did. Now it's time for us to leave.'

'I know what you *said*, but . . .' Sian groped for words to express her indignation, and came to a baffled pause.

Annabel couldn't help sympathising, she knew so exactly what her daughter was trying to say. So much seemed to have happened since her grudging promise of the night before last. She'd agreed only to bring them here, but things had changed since then. Or seemed to have changed, more fool her.

'Can't you see, darling?' she tried to explain. 'We'd be . . . in the way here now.'

'No, we wouldn't, there's heaps of room.'

'It isn't space, it's . . . privacy. Your father's got a . . . a lady-friend here now . . .'

'*You're* his lady-friend.'

'I'm not . . .'

'You *are!*' The small jaw was set, the tender mouth tight. 'But even if you weren't . . . I'm not going.'

'You are, you know.' Annabel spoke softly,

almost with compassion. She always won this
kind of argument; she had to. She only wished the
child wouldn't waste her strength, refusing to
accept the inevitable.

Still, there it was, Sian wasn't going to give in
with-out a fight, and this time she thought she had
an ally. 'You can go by yourself. I'll stay here with
Daddy.'

'You can't do that, darling.'

'Can't I? Let's see.'

A whirl of displaced air, a light patter of feet
along the corridor and down the stairs, and she
was gone. She'd be seeking her father's support,
poor scrap, and this time she'd be disappointed.
He wouldn't want even her about the place now.
He might offer some consolation, suggest they
come back in a day or two—and he'd be told what
he could do with that, Annabel thought fiercely as
she checked the room for anything she might have
left out of her packing. Once clear of this place
which had witnessed her weakening and her
humiliation, she was never coming back.

Not to it and not to Caird. How dared he talk of
settling in Rybridge? With Becky, he must have
meant, planning his future with another woman
and talking as if it mattered as much to herself as to
him. Bone selfish, that's what he was, a complete
egoist, and she was a fool ever to have believed
any different. Reckoning to have his girl and his
daughter, and never stopping to consider the
misery he might bring to . . . anybody else,
anybody who might be forced to observe his
happiness with his Becky as a new, horrible part of

their daily lives.

But she wouldn't be miserable. He wasn't worth being miserable over. Annabel sniffed hard, and had to open the overnight bag to find her tissues. And blowing her nose made her eyes water, so she'd have to mop them, too. Another tissue, and still the flowers in the windowbox blurred again. She blinked hard, and looked down over the sunlit hillside to where the church raised its serene onion dome over the roofs of the village. This place had seemed so peaceful, so right, she had been so much looking forward to—but she mustn't let herself think like that. She heard light footsteps behind her, and prepared to comfort Sian who would now have been disillusioned in her turn.

But it wasn't Sian. It was Becky

Annabel gulped and drew herself up, wondering and refusing to let herself wonder what the girl wanted. It was the lightness of the tread which had deceived her, the perfectly balanced suppleness of the young and agile. And this girl was very young, grey eyes lively as spring clouds in the unlined face.

'Your daughter,' she began at once, 'she's upset.'

Annabel turned abruptly away. 'We're all upset. And now . . .'

She looked round for something to do, some way of elbowing the girl out of her attention. But Becky would not be elbowed. She strolled to the bed, dumped the overnight bag on the floor, and sat down, clearly prepared for a long and serious discussion. Annabel looked out of the window again.

'Yeah, well,' the voice began, 'I was a bit miffed myself, when I heard who you were.'

'You needn't worry. We'll . . .'

'But I don't see *your* angle,' the voice went on placidly. 'What's bugging you?'

Annabel spun back to look, unable to believe the evidence of her ears alone. To be free of jealousy yourself was one thing; to be so free of it you couldn't understand it in others, that had to be an act. Yet it didn't seem to be. The lithe young figure was completely relaxed, legs in a gracefully inelegant sprawl, wide forehead calm and unruffled, clear eyes meeting hers with a cool, detached interest. There was something familiar about those eyes. Not the colour, not the shape—and yet, there was something.

'After all,' Becky was reasoning now, 'if I can forget it, surely you can?'

'We must be made differently,' Annabel snapped.

Becky frowned a small, passing frown, then shrugged. 'OK. Seems like you're set on going. Poor Pa . . .'

'Pa?' Annabel stood very still. 'What are you talking about?'

'Damned if I can see why he wants *you* to stay . . .' The emphasis Becky put on the 'you' made it clear she meant Annabel rather than Sian, and she went on to express herself even more freely, 'You finished off his marriage, you wouldn't let him help bring up his own daughter . . .'

'I did what?'

Seeing her bewilderment, Becky explained, 'You

sure gave Ma that last little push, bustin' in as if you owned the place . . .'

'I . . . didn't know . . .'

But Becky wasn't concerned with Annabel's side of it. 'Ma wanted to talk to him about this job,' she went on, lost in her troubled childhood, 'see if he'd go with her, free-lance again. She was hopin' they could get back together, till she saw you . . . Hey, there!' She leapt to her feet. 'You OK?'

Annabel opened her eyes, glad of the strong young arm that had come so quickly to her aid. She found something familiar in that, too, and now she knew why. She looked into the wide grey eyes. They weren't Caird's eyes—the girl must take after her mother—but they had Caird's very expression, Sian's, too—open, direct, interested.

'Come and sit down.'

Becky helped her to the bed, and she was glad to be helped. All the stiffening seemed to have gone out of her bones, her muscles, her mind—she felt as if she'd just been put through a mincer. When she spoke again, it was softly, uncertainly.

'He says . . .' She licked dry lips, knowing this calm, downright girl could be trusted to answer one of the questions plaguing her. 'He says he was divorced before we ever met.'

'When was that?' Becky asked.

'Ten years ago last month.'

Head on one side, Becky did some calculations. 'I guess that's right, then.'

Annabel heaved a sigh of relief. Caird had told the truth about his marriage.

'And so you're his d-daughter?'

'Why, sure,' Becky sounded mildly amused, 'what else, would you think?'

Annabel swallowed hard. She wasn't going to say what else. 'I mean,' Becky went on, 'what would I be doin' here in the bondooks with a guy that old?'

'He's only thirty-seven . . .'

'An' the fellas back in Vienna cryin' into their mochas,' Becky warmed to her theme. 'They're all goin' down to the Old Danube this weekend, to windsurf.'

Annabel nodded, understanding the attraction of youth to youth. 'And you gave that up so you could visit your father?'

'Guess I'm kinda sorry for him,' Becky agreed. 'Looks to me like he's kinda lonely.'

Lonely. Annabel closed her eyes again, trying to adapt to this new picture of the famous journalist, womaniser, sophisticated traveller.

'Well, maybe not,' Becky conceded. 'After all, there's you. Or there was, before you started . . .'

'Where's Sian?' Annabel asked, reminded of her daughter's unhappiness.

'Helpin' Pa carry wood for the stove. I think he figured it'd cool her off.'

Yes, some undemanding practical task like that would be exactly what Sian needed now. Annabel was impressed again at how well Caird seemed able to deal with his daughter. His younger daughter, she corrected herself, trying to get used to it. She regarded Becky with curiosity.

'How old are you?'

'Eighteen. Ma wanted me to go to UCLA, but I

said no. Not yet, anyway.'

'UCLA?'

'University of California, Los Angles,' Becky explained, with mild pity for the outsider who didn't understand such things. 'I'll get round to it by and by. Maybe.'

'Why there?'

'You didn't know that, either?' The grey eyes surveyed her with that calm open stare. 'That job Ma took—it was in California. We went that summer, right after she'd been to see Pa.'

Annabel's head was spinning again. 'California,' she repeated stupidly. 'And you must have been eight . . .'

'Damn right I was. An' that was the end of Pa 'n' me, till now.'

'You mean,' Annabel paused, not wanting to believe it, 'you never met again?'

'Oh, we met. It just . . . wasn't the same. You know how it is.'

Annabel didn't know how it was, but could imagine. Supposing someone had been allowed by law to take Sian to the other side of the world, letting them meet only on certain set occasions. It would be unbearable. Even the meetings would be unbearable, so eagerly awaited, so strained, so painful with reminders of the ever-widening gap between yourself and this growing stranger who had once been part of you. No wonder Caird had been so determined to hang on to Sian. No wonder he'd sometimes talked about her with such hopeless longing. The longing was indeed hopeless, for what would most satisfy it—the childhood of his other child—was gone, never to return.

And it had been her fault. Annabel faced it squarely, disliking what she saw, disliking herself but determined to know the worst about herself. She'd been so blinded by her own needs, she'd taken it for granted he was all hers, there for her whenever she wanted him, any time of day she could free herself to find again the comfort she needed in his body and his being. His gentleness, his strength, his understanding—she'd wanted them, so they had to be hers. It had simply never occurred to her that other things in his life might matter just as much to him. Like the daughter she hadn't known about, who had been taken by his angry wife to the other side of the world, directly after her own over-confident interruption that day.

'He—he never told me about you.'

She wasn't trying to excuse herself, only exclaiming in sheer misery as it all came back to her. Of course he hadn't. It must have been a painful experience, breaking up a marriage and losing a beloved child, and in those days she was the last person anyone would go to for sympathy. She hadn't been interested, hadn't considered anybody else's troubles, was always wrapped up in her own. He must have looked for an opening, just as he had been waiting for it on this journey.

She squirmed as she remembered the way she had let herself dismiss his broken marriage, never doubting that his weakness had been the cause, when all the time . . . she winced. When all the time, the weakness which robbed him of his daughter had been her own.

'I guess Ma would've gone, anyway,' Becky admitted. 'It was a great job, she loves the research she's doin' now. I'd have liked them back together, but . . .' She sighed, dismissing the past. 'To think of you having that cute little girl. My sister.'

'I can see the resemblance,' Annabel said, and she could. Both girls were slender, strong, confident, at ease within their bodies. Looking at the freckled, straight-nosed profile beside her, she reflected that she would be proud if Sian grew up as nice as this.

The profile turned towards her, and the grey eyes met hers again in that direct Gloster gaze. 'Pa says you're awful set on your own way, once you take an idea.'

'H-he's been talking about me, then?'

'Well, he had to, hadn't he? To explain Sian and all.'

'Yes.' Annabel remembered her jealous rage when Becky had been whisked into the kitchen. Yet again she'd been wrong, never once stopped to ask a question, just thought she knew it all and gone on from there.

'Yes,' she said again. 'Of course.'

Of course it was Becky who needed the explanations, finding herself suddenly presented with a sister of Sian's age.

'What—what else did he say?' she was unable to resist the question.

'Why, that it was like . . . having a second chance.' Becky's brow furrowed as she tried to recall her father's words. 'That now he'd got it, he was damn well gonna hang on to it.'

'Meaning Sian?'

'Why, yes. Us breakin' up the way we did.'

Annabel's heart twisted again. Of course it was Sian he wanted, how could it be otherwise? For Sian's sake, he would accept Sian's difficult mother, put up with her barbed comments, her conviction that she knew all there was to know, her willingness to assume the worst and fly into a rage about it.

She had a sudden, vivid recollection of their first conversation, on the boat. He'd only once allowed himself a comment on what she had become, and even that had been more in depression than anger, when he'd said, 'It's worse than I thought.'

She knew what he meant now, but at the time she'd hardly noticed. Any more than she had when he'd told her to stop making silly, smart remarks and just try listening for a change.

She hadn't listened, not then, not later. Instead, she'd gone for him whenever she could, small and snappy and sure of her grievances, never thinking for a moment that he, too, might have cause to regret having known her. And he'd taken it all, never once let her provoke him into retaliating with the simple truth, that, thanks to her, his other daughter was being brought up thousands of miles beyond his reach. He'd never told her that or anything like it, not even during his initial anger—the only time she had seen him angry— when he first saw Sian. She could well understand that anger now. She had robbed him, not of one daughter, but of two.

Annabel swallowed hard. All her fierce pride went down in one big gulp, and left her humble, uncertain, not knowing what to say. Luckily, Becky saved her the trouble.

'I came up to ask, won't you change your mind?'

'I . . . er . . .' Annabel met the open grey gaze, swallowed again, and abandoned any attempt to explain. 'I have.'

'Why, that's great!' Becky lit up with a delighted smile—no doubt at all, she meant it.

Encouraged, Annabel rushed on, 'I—I . . . look, I need some time alone with your father, and Sian wants to go to the livery stables. D'you think . . .'

'Why, sure, I'll take her,' Becky agreed warmly. 'It'll be a chance for us sisters to get acquainted.'

She made for the door, and after a brief hesitation Annabel followed.

CHAPTER TEN

BECKY announced the change of plan before they'd reached the foot of the stairs. Sian was by the stove, adding a log to the pile drying there, and glanced up with a frown as if she heard but couldn't take it in. Then she dropped her log with a thump and pelted across, so Annabel stepped from the bottom stair into an ecstatic hug and a disjointed demand to be told was it true, were they staying, was she sure? It was, they were, she was, she managed to answer and was busy enough not to be too flustered when Caird came in with another log and an enquiring look.

Luckily, the scene explained itself. It was Caird's reaction which worried her. He was pleased—wasn't he? Pleased, yes, but with certain reservations. In the short time it took for Becky to collect Sian and set off with her down the hill, Annabel was uneasier than ever before with him.

It was like being left alone with a stranger. And yet, as they waved their daughters off from the gate of the courtyard and returned in silence to the living-room, Annabel knew she loved this stranger. Loved him more than she ever had, and knew as she had never known before how unworthy she was of being loved in return. Becky's cool comment—'damned if I can see why he wants you'—came back to her. He doesn't, she thought, he's only putting up with me for Sian's sake.

He gestured at the table, back now in its usual place. The half-burnt candles were gone, but their very absence reminded her of the way he had coped with the power-cut last night, and borne her grouchiness along with his own worries. All right, so she'd been tired, but that was her own silly fault for thinking she could drive so far. That was the whole story of this journey—her blaming him and sounding off whenever she felt like it, him coping without fuss, keeping always to his main purpose of protecting and caring for her and Sian. Her cheap cracks about his past must have hurt him, angered him too, yet never once had he retaliated, as he so well could have done, with the truth. She took her place at the table and waited for him to settle beside her, unable to face his quizzical glance.

'What's it all been about, love?'

'I . . . I . . .' She gulped down the last of that destructive pride and got it out fast. 'I-thought-she-was-your-girlfriend.'

'What?' He was astonished, amused, incredulous. 'So that's why you flew off the deep end?'

'You wouldn't talk about her . . .'

'Touching wood, love.' Caird sobered abruptly. 'I'm just getting her back after all the years. It wouldn't do to take anything for granted.'

Annabel stared ahead, understanding so well that she ached for him. 'Is that why you bought this place?'

'As soon as I knew she was coming here to practise the language,' he confirmed, smiling, 'I knew she'd want to help me do it up. She's got a bossy streak,' the smile was fond, 'like Millie.' Sombre again, he went on slowly, 'You know, love, I still feel a failure over that marriage.'

'As if you ever could be. And . . . ' She looked across the years at her younger self, conscious of how little she had helped him in his unhappiness. 'I can see exactly why you didn't talk to me about it. All I did was rush in and lose you Becky . . .'

'Rubbish!'

Taken aback by the flat contradiction, she stared, and saw how deep it was etched into him, the bitterness she had noticed so often.

'Becky's had ten years to see things her mother's way . . .' He bit off the comment, then went on evenly, 'I'd better . . . give you my side.'

She waited, breathless, to hear him speak of it at last.

'We . . . married too young.'

He paused again, and she was aware of the struggle within him, the unhappy memories he was putting into words with such difficulty. She tried to help him.

'You must have been . . . about the age Becky is now?'

'Starting college. And . . . the baby wasn't intentional.'

She met his eyes, saddened to think how hard she had made it for him to tell her this earlier. Two days ago, she would have seized the chance to score, taunted him with his male carelessness . . . but she could at least listen now.

'The best way for everybody seemed to be if I dropped out of college, and free-lanced from home. Home . . .' He looked beyond her, reminiscing. 'Two rooms and use of kitchen.'

'You, too,' she murmured, trying to take it in. 'You had to struggle, looking after a baby and working, same as I did . . .'

'Millie did her share. But she was a scientist, she had to finish her course. And then she got a research fellowship . . .'

Annabel was silent, filling in what he left out. Millie absorbed in her work, Caird at home, a widening gulf between. And, at the same time, in the daily feeding and nursing and teaching and loving, he must have come ever closer to his daughter.

'They were great,' he went on, 'those years with Becky. When we finally . . . admitted defeat on our marriage . . . I fought for custody. Millie won.'

Annabel sat quite still. Once more she was longing to put her arms round him, kiss away the lines of pain she now understood so well, but she dared not. She hadn't the right.

'By then I was researching the programme, travelling a lot—I couldn't look after Becky full-time. Neither could Millie.'

'What did you do?'

'Asked my parents to take her till we sorted something out. They were delighted . . .' He turned to look down at her. 'That's where it stood when I met you.'

'And . . . I was no help.'

'How could I invite you into a messed-up life

like mine?'

'Is that . . . ' She returned his look with amazement. 'It that what you were thinking of?'

'All the time, my darling.' He stared at her hungrily. 'It wasn't just your looks, it wasn't just your . . . passion. It was . . . whatever it is that's *you*. Only——' he broke off in exasperation '—it wouldn't have been fair to you.'

'I . . . I didn't know you felt like that,' she said, and added, from her new knowledge of herself, 'I don't think I cared much about how you felt. Only about me.'

'You were so young. So unhappy . . . and then Millie arrived, to talk about the job in California.'

'Becky says she asked you to go with her.'

'She did. Becky was only eight, remember—still needed a lot of care. And the new job was even more round-the-clock.'

'And that's why Millie wanted you? Because of your help with Becky?'

'It wasn't that simple.' He shrugged, helpless. 'I think maybe she was . . . missing me, too, by then.'

'Could be.' Annabel devoured him with her eyes, wondering how any woman could ever have let him go. 'But anyway, you were about to get your own programme, weren't you? That was a lot to give up.'

'It had to be considered, certainly. I was trying to work out what would be best for all of us . . . when you walked in. End of discussion.'

'So it *was* my fault . . .'

'No!' Caird shook his head vigorously.

'But Millie took her away . . .'

'Millie . . . did what she wanted, love.'

The admission seemed torn out of him, and she loved him more than ever for his restraint. He wouldn't blame his ex-wife, that was one reason why he was having such trouble telling the story. He was seeing both sides of it, not just putting himself in the right. And yet, what misery lay behind those words! In that one brief confrontation of the two women in his life, he had lost what mattered to him more than either—his two daughters.

At last she could suffer with him the pain he had so often tried to conceal from her. He was admitting it now, and in the fullness of her love she could take his hand, stroke his hair, try with her closeness to make up a little of what he had lost. But so little. And she could have given him so much. But for her wretched pride and her belief that she knew it all, she could have given him Sian right from babyhood.

He turned to her with more love than she could ever deserve. 'So that was it. Millie gone, Becky gone, you gone . . . was it bad, managing on your own?'

'Yes,' she admitted, barely above a whisper, 'until Sian was born. After that . . . like it was with you . . .'

'Looking after Becky, you mean?'

She nodded, fearful of the memories she must be stirring in him. 'However hard things were, she was worth it all.'

'Oh, my dear!'

She looked at the play of the sun on the scrubbed tabletop. 'You said that once before, like that. On the boat. What . . . what did it mean?

'Your courage. Your strength . . .'

'My . . .'

'I've seen it right through this journey, just like it used to be, only . . . you're a woman now.'

'So you really . . .' she raised her head wonderingly, unable to believe it ' . . . really like me?'

His laugh sounded shaky. 'What more can I do to prove it?'

'It's so hard to believe.'

'Not from where I'm sitting.' He paused, and went on softly, 'Have you thought about what I said last night?'

'About you coming to live in Rybridge?'

'Doing it like that, Sian could stay at her school, and you at your business.' He warmed to his theme. 'We could make it work, I'm sure we could . . .'

'Er . . .' she gave him a demure sideways look '. . . make *what* work?'

'And just think—for the next baby, I'd be right with you all the time . . .'

'Caird Gloster, aren't you forgetting something?'

'Am I?'

'The next baby!' She giggled, suddenly light-hearted. 'And you've never even mentioned marriage.'

'Haven't I?' He blinked, paused, frowned. 'But surely you knew that was what I meant?'

'How could I, when I was worrying about Becky?

And you wouldn't make love . . .'

'My darling, you were tired out of your mind. That's no way to make decisons such as, shall we have another baby . . .'

He slowed down and stopped. She had slipped a foot out of her sandal, and was nestling it against his ankle.

'Am I allowed to decide now?' she asked. 'Sian says we need a double bed, and here it is.'

'Oh, no, you, don't, Annabel Blythe!' Caird seized her hand, which had strayed to caress the line of his jaw. 'You did that to me once, drove me out of my mind with wanting you . . .' he grabbed her other hand, which was unbuttoning his shirt ' . . . and then ran away. This time you're going to make an honest man of me . . .'

She closed her eyes to enjoy sweetness of his lips in her palms. 'Supposing you just try asking?'

'All right. Annabel Blythe, will you marry me?'

'Yes, my darling,' she spoke in a trembling whisper, freeing her hands to draw him close. 'Yes, I'll marry you. Now, about that double bed . . .'

Slowly, he stood up. Then, just as he had last night, he pulled back the table, picked her up, and swung her across the huge room, while she opened his shirt further and nestled one hand in the hair of his chest.

While he went to lock the door, she dealt with her clothes. The olive-green blouse and jeans fell away like an empty shell, and she was open and vulnerable as she had been long ago, pushing back the duvet and rejoicing in his hungry eyes that lingered on every line and curve of her body.

'You, too,' she whispered, and watched the shirt drop from his broad shoulders, the jeans from his narrow hips. It was in her view again for the first time in ten years, that marvellous male fire rearing from his loins. She cradled it in her hands, exulting and confident because she knew at last that it was hers and only.

'My beloved, headlong Annabel,' he murmured, sinking beside her and pushing her back to the softness of the bed. 'But we're going the slow way.'

'The slow way.' She remembered the phrase from long ago, and offered him her breasts.

'The pretty way.' His voice came out muffled, his lips trailing and tantalising until she moaned in protest and they closed on one jutting peak. She gasped and shuddered, knowing his moulding tongue wouldn't leave there until it had driven her to a frenzy.

'Please,' she gasped. 'It's been so long . . .'

She drew his head from her breast and sought his lips with her own. In the depth of that drowning, endless kiss, she felt herself close triumphantly round him, felt her emptiness filled to overflowing, filled and blossoming like a flower whose endless tendrils spread and wrapped her round until nothing else existed, nothing mattered but rhythm, the heat, the certainty of a man and a woman joined where they were made to be joined, and sliding together towards ecstasy.

She had known it so often in her dreams, this ecstasy, but now it was different. This was no weightless phantom lover, but Caird, real and solid above her, hard-muscled chest against her breasts, hard belly against hers, hard thighs so intermingled with her own she couldn't tell and didn't care where she left off and he began. Together they drove throught the hot waves of passion, together rose to their crest, where time and space and earth and heaven shattered and mingled to whirling, brilliant darkness.

And when it all came back, when the world had settled round her again in its accustomed shapes, he was still there. His head was beside hers on the pillow, his hands smoothed her hips and her belly and her shoulder, drew her to him and murmured the tender, broken phrases her dreams could never supply.

'Were you pleased?' she asked sleepily.

'Very, very pleased, my darling. But next time,' he nibbled her ear in punishment for her disobedience, 'we go the slow way.'

'And when will next time be?' Her fingers had located his heartbeat, and she rose on one elbow to set her lips against it. From there, it seemed only natural to seize the hair of his chest in her teeth and tug gently, then to curl her tongue round his nipple, to find out if it tasted as good as it had ten years ago.

Caird drew a sharp breath. 'My dear, sweet witch, you're trying to cheat again!' He wrapped his fingers in her hair and tugged gently. 'It's my turn first.'

'Those were the old rules. I've changed them.'

'All right. But you still have to let me look at

you. I have to look at you, Bel. You're so beautiful
. . .'

As he spoke, he gently lifted her hands from his
body, kicked the duvet to the foot of the bed, and
moved away from her. She shivered and closed
her eyes, feeling his gaze like an invisible caress on
the length of her legs, the narrowness of her waist,
the enfolding richness of her thighs. Yes, like this
and for him she *was* beautiful, she knew now it
was true.

'You shine.' He was touching her inner thigh
with just one finger. 'You shine like a pearl.'

'It's being loved by you. Love me again, Caird.'

'I will, my darling, I will.'

She felt his lips on her belly, his tongue in her
navel, and then heard a car arriving in the
courtyard. He sat up at once, alert and ready for
action as ever, and she relished the small chill he
had left behind, the tiny parting that would end so
soon in unity and fullness.

'Who is it?' she asked as he leapt out of bed,
'The girls were on foot . . .'

'It's Otto, about the elecricity.'

Too happy to be disconcerted, she stretched like
a kitten and watched him through her lashes,
savouring his height and his power and the quick,
deft movements that hid the clean lines of his body
in crumpled shirt and trousers. While he tidied his
hair, she remembered the power supply seemed to
be back in order.

'I thought he'd fixed it?'

'No, it just came on. It does that sometimes.' He
leant to kiss her shoulder. 'He has a key, but I'll

head him off.'

Annabel looked up at him through half-closed eyes. 'Will he guess why?'

'Probably. But in any case, I'll tell him . . .' He pulled down the cover and lingered over her breasts, tantalising and denying them, with his lips just out of their reach. She laughed and reared up, but he won the game, kept his distance, and would allow her no more than the quick promise of his tongue on each.

He straightened and grinned at her over the new demand he had so easily created, the rosy peaks thrusting up for the touch he had refused them.

'. . . I'll tell him,' he repeated as he made for the door, 'that we've lots of electricity already.'

🔷 Harlequin Superromance

**Here are the longer, more involving stories you
have been waiting for . . . Superromance.**

Modern, believable novels of love, full of the complex
joys and heartaches of real people.

Intriguing conflicts based on today's constantly
changing life-styles.

Four new titles every month.
Available wherever paperbacks are sold.

Keepsake

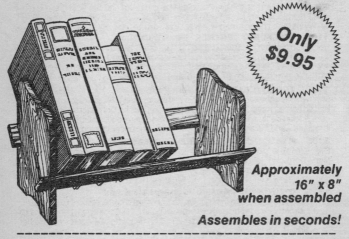

Harlequin Presents

Coming Next Month

Available in March wherever paperback books are sold, or through
Harlequin Reader Service:

In the U.S.
901 Fuhrmann Blvd.
P.O. Box 1397
Buffalo, N.Y. 14240-1397

In Canada
P.O. Box 603
Fort Erie, Ontario
L2A 5X3